NINE DAYS TO KILL

NINE DAYS TO KILL

JULIE ELLIS

G.K. Hall & Co. • Chivers Press
Thorndike, Maine USA Bath, England

This Large Print edition is published by G.K. Hall & Co., USA
and by Chivers Press, England.

Published in 1997 in the U.S. by arrangement with
Chivers Press Limited.

Published in 1997 in the U.K. by arrangement with
Severn House Publishers Ltd.

U.S.   Softcover   0-7838-8078-2   (Paperback Collection Edition)
U.K.   Hardcover   0-7451-8969-5   (Chivers Large Print)
U.K.   Softcover   0-7451-8971-7   (Camden Large Print)

The text of this Large Print edition is unabridged.
Other aspects of the book may vary from the original edition.

Set in 16 pt. Plantin by Al Chase.

Printed in the United States on permanent paper.

British Library Cataloguing in Publication Data available

Library of Congress Cataloging in Publication Data

Ellis, Julie, 1933–
    Nine days to kill / Julie Ellis.
      p.   cm.
    ISBN 0-7838-8078-2 (lg. print : sc)
    1. Large type books.   I. Title.
    [PS3555.L597N5 1997]
    813'.54—dc21   96-53539

NINE DAYS TO KILL

Prologue

In skintight black leather slacks and a white cotton Yves St Laurent shirt, his feet in Gucci loafers, Randall Brooks stood before Anita Cantrell's tooled leather desk in the large, high-ceilinged, magnificently furnished library of her duplex penthouse co-op, high over Fifth Avenue in the East Seventies. Her brusque dismissal of their torrid affair echoed in his brain — he stared at her in disbelief as she leaned forward to pick up her chequebook.

"Anita, what the hell are you talking about?" His voice shook with rage. It couldn't be happening this way. Not after all his plans. All his work. This was his ultimate campaign. "After the way it's been for us? Don't you remember, Anita?" He leaned across the desk, switching on the magnetic Randall Brooks charm. One hand fondled her arm. "Anita, baby —"

"Randall, it's over." She pulled her arm away. Her face was taut, determined. Her hand was unsteady as she reached for a pen. "You saw the subpoena." Her eyes rested for a distasteful instant on the legal document at one corner of the desk. "My mother is suing me for custody of Larry. If she wins this suit, she'll have control of Larry's trust fund instead of me! I'm flying down to Palm Beach tomorrow to talk to her."

"But you'll be coming back," he protested.

"Randall, it's over." She refused to meet his eyes. "I can't afford to take chances. Mother's rotten detectives know all about you." And about all the other men in Anita's hectic social life, Randall guessed subconsciously. "I must convince her I'm living like a nun now. That her case won't stand up in court." He felt the wall jutting up between them. "Don't beat it to death, Randall."

"I don't believe you!" His struggled to control himself. His instinct was to smash his fist into her beautiful face — a masterpiece contrived by a series of expensive plastic surgeons. "You can't do this to me!" So she'd lose control of the trust fund. She had a fortune in her own right. Nobody threw over Randall Brooks. He walked out when he was through with a chick. That was the way it'd always been. "Anita, last Friday night —" he tried again. "Don't you remember?" He was a twenty-four-year old stud who knew how to make a thirty-nine-year-old twice analysed, thrice divorced jet-setter go right up the wall. For a moment his confidence returned. "You'll be back from Palm Beach right after New Year's. It'll be like it always was!"

In the five months that he had been sleep-in help for the Cantrells — butler and chauffeur, he had come to relish this fancy living. Anita knew he wasn't a domestic. She had picked him up on the beach at East Hampton, where he was playing the beach bum scene, not long after the kid Larry went blind.

She had just fired the chauffeur for pilfering. He'd told Anita right off that he was a UCLA drop-out — she knew his potential when he finally decided to settle down. Hell, he could hold his own beside her any day.

Damn it, he wanted this set up. Anita Cantrell was a great-looking broad, even if she was thirty-nine. And more importantly, she was rich. He had been sure he had it made. This was the jackpot.

"Randall, I'm giving you four weeks' severance pay," she said, as coolly as though they had never wrestled up a sweat together beneath those fancy silk sheets in her bedroom and which travelled with her wherever she went. "Five months is a long time for you to stay any place. You said so yourself." Now her hazel eyes met his with impersonal calm.

"You'll hate yourself for this," he warned, trying to mask panic with charm. The chauffeur at the Hamptons had been dumped not for pilferage, Martha — the housekeeper-cook — had confided, but because Anita's six-year-old kid had seen something he shouldn't have. Larry couldn't see now. The doctors talked about 'hysterical blindness', Anita said, without enlarging on it. Like his seeing Anita and the guy having a ball? "Anita, baby, you need me," he tried again, reaching for her hand. "Look, if it'll make it easier to keep the kid, why don't we get married?"

Anita stared at him as though she had never

truly seen him before. With a contempt that turned him to ice.

"Randall, don't be naîve." She ripped the cheque from the book with an air of finality. "Finish up this afternoon, then clear out. I want those drapes hung in the library before you leave."

"Yes, Madam," he said bitterly. His head was beginning to ache, he realized in irritation. He had not had a bad headache in months. Anita's fault, damn her.

Chapter One

Kathy Anderson, southbound on the Henry Hudson Parkway in the deep gloom of this pre-Christmas afternoon, watched for the 79th Street turn-off. The earth and asphalt were dampened by an intermittent drizzle that threatened to become sleet or snow. The trees that dotted the landscape were depressingly gaunt. The ground winter-barren.

Nervously she inspected the grey-red sky. But no need to worry, she soothed herself. If the snow was heavy enough to stick tonight, the gritters would be out on the road.

What an unexpected way to be spending the Christmas holidays! But when Mrs Cantrell phoned yesterday — after that strange call from the employment agency — and indicated what she was willing to pay, she knew she would accept this short assignment. She'd thought that once she had her Master's in Special Education she'd walk right into a teaching job. But not in this rotten recession, she taunted herself with recurrent frustration. The economists might say the recession was over — but for all those hunting for jobs that was the joke of the century.

Robin was upset that she refused to fly out to Texas for the holidays.

"Kathy, you're all the family I have, except for

Joe and the kids," her sister had reminded. "We'll send you the plane tickets. Nobody's going to be hiring at a time like this."

She couldn't bring herself to face Robin's questions about Clint. For five months her whole life had revolved about him, as Robin knew — until he had laid it on the line four weeks ago.

"Baby, I hate living this way." He shared a decrepit apartment with two other grad students near the Columbia campus. She was in the family house in Tarrytown and scrounging to survive until her parents' estate was out of probate — or a job came up. "I want somebody on a full-time basis. Let's move in together — either your house or something we can find near school — or let's split."

Her face tightened. He wasn't talking marriage — just living together. She wasn't ready for that kind of lifestyle. Not after the trauma of these past seven months. Sometimes she felt she was living a nightmare — and she'd wake up and she'd find her parents were alive. But the plane crash that killed them had been real. Breaking up with Clint had left a painful hole in her life. She realized now that she wasn't in love with Clint. She'd been grieving and lonely, and he had helped her cope during these painful months. They'd shared a strong common interest — a dedication to work with troubled children — though their motives were different. Her heart reached out to these kids. Clint saw them as the road to affluent living. Once he had his doctorate he hoped to open up a school for disturbed kids. *Rich* disturbed kids. And she wondered if part of her attraction was that she would be half-owner of a large house in Tarrytown that could serve as quarters for a small school. *But what she'd felt for Clint had not been love.*

Kathy straightened up behind the wheel. The turn-off was just ahead. She flipped the indicator and switched lanes, followed the car ahead off the parkway to circle onto the Manhattan street. Cut left, her mind ordered, then drive through Central Park to the east side of the city.

For a few minutes Kathy focused on driving in unfamiliar territory. She rarely drove into Manhattan — usually she took the train. But she'd need Mom's car if she was to take this brief, weird job.

She headed east, toward the park, remembering to be careful about taking the right routes lest she wind up on Central Park South instead of Fifth Avenue. Relieved when she was at last driving south on Fifth Avenue. Traffic was bumper-to-bumper, moving sluggishly the day before Christmas Eve. Despite the recession and tight money New Yorkers were surging into the stores for last-minute shopping. Buses, heavy with passengers, clogged the avenue.

She watched for the street where she was to make the turn-off to the garage. No need to worry about available space. When Mrs Cantrell called yesterday, she said she would arrange for this.

Kathy waited with strained patience for traffic

to move. In her mind she heard Mrs Cantrell's tense, affected voice: "I realize this is awfully short notice, but I must fly down to Palm Beach day after tomorrow to spend the holidays with my mother. I had expected Larry's father — he was my second husband — to be home to take Larry for the holidays. But at the last moment David cabled that he'll be held up in Rio on his current engineering assignment. Larry was afflicted with this terrible, strange blindness almost eight months ago. He's being tutored at home, but his tutor will be on vacation as of tomorrow. Someone must be with him constantly in his condition."

"When will you be back?" Kathy had asked. "I'm trying to set up interviews for —"

"Oh, I'll be back the day after New Year's," Mrs Cantrell had interrupted impatiently. "I want you to take Larry up to this private school in Salem, New York, and stay with him till New Year's day. That's no problem, is it?" Irritation lent stridency to her voice now.

"No," Kathy reassured her. She needed the money Mrs Cantrell offered for this service.

"It's magnificent country, right on the Vermont border. The house was built in 1831 and is completely restored," Mrs Cantrell rattled on in obvious relief. "It's on a hundred acre farm well out of town, with nothing in sight except fields and mountains. With you at his side, Kathy," Anita Cantrell's voice became consciously ingratiating, "Larry can ice-skate and go sledding. He can have

14

the companionship of the other children staying at the school for the holidays."

But why wasn't Mrs Cantrell taking her son with her to visit his grandmother? Poor little kid — to be sloughed on off a stranger at Christmas. Like those other kids at the school. How could parents have so little sense of responsibility?

Kathy brushed her lush dark hair away from her delicately featured face. Her blue eyes checked the sky again. She'd be nervous driving in heavy snow, but there was no direct plane, train, or bus connection to Salem. Besides, Mrs Cantrell expected her to drive. She'd need a car up there. It would be their only means of transportation.

Inching along in the frustrating stop-and-go traffic, Kathy sorted out the information Mrs Cantrell had given her in the twenty minute telephone interview. Larry had become blind suddenly. Unseeing, he had stumbled into the pool at their summer house at East Hampton and would have drowned if a delivery man had not arrived at just that moment and pulled him out.

The school to which she was taking Larry catered to learning disabled children. Bright, happy children, Mrs Cantrell had insisted in her tense, high-pitched voice. But they had difficulty in learning. Five of them were remaining at the school over the holidays because their parents — for one reason or another — were not bringing them home. One was a child of a friend of Anita Cantrell. This was how she had made the arrangements to have Larry spend the holidays at the school.

Already the drizzle was turning into sleet. Two hundred miles of driving lay ahead of her. Mrs Cantrell had specified that Larry and she were to leave immediately after an early dinner this evening. This way Larry would sleep most of the trip up to the school.

Her tyres were good, Kathy comforted herself. The car was in good condition, bought three weeks before Mom and Dad crashed in the plane that was taking them to see Robin's new baby. Tears stung Kathy's eyes. Her first Christmas without Mom and Dad.

These past five months Clint had pulled her out of the grief that had coloured her life since that awful telephone call. But she wasn't ready for the kind of relationship Clint demanded. She wasn't ready to marry Clint, either, she thought with honesty. At unnerving intervals she felt as though she was waiting for something. Without knowing for what she waited.

On the side street Kathy found the garage where Mrs Cantrell had reserved parking space. She handed over the keys to an attendant that looked astonishingly like Clint, and for a moment she was cold with longing.

No! That was all over. Clint had become a habit with her. Somebody to whom she could cling. She was not in love with him. She'd been lonely and scared and unsure of herself.

She left the garage, fished in one pocket of her

plum down coat for gloves, in another pocket for the matching wool ski cap. Mom's last present — after they'd perused a mail order catalogue together. What rotten, depressing weather! Her shoulders hunched with distaste she walked in the direction of Fifth Avenue. Despite the traffic she would arrive right on schedule, she thought with relief. She loathed being late for appointments.

In a few moments she was inside the cozy warmth of the elegant apartment building and riding up to the penthouse. At the door to the apartment she fought down a wave of self-consciousness. Why did she suddenly feel a strange foreboding? As though she was about to leap into dark, forbidding, unchartered territory. Oh, it was absurd to feel this way! It was just because this job had happened so fast. But Mrs Bevans at the agency had recommended her, Kathy reminded herself — and Mrs Cantrell had little time to make a choice.

Kathy touched the doorbell. She heard the musical chimes inside. The rich pile of the beige carpeting beneath her feet was oddly reassuring. The wallpaper in the foyer — exclusively at the disposal of the two penthouse residents — was exquisite and expensive. Such wealth as the Cantrells enjoyed, Kathy thought wryly, was foreign to her.

A uniformed maid opened the door and ushered her inside. Mrs Cantrell was waiting for her in the family sitting room, the maid explained, and led the way.

17

A coldly beautiful, bone-thin woman in a red velvet designer caftan — perhaps three inches taller than Kathy's slim five feet three — strode towards her with a brittle smile.

"Hi, Kathy," Anita Cantrell greeted her with artificial warmth. "You look exactly as I expected. So pretty and vivacious. Mrs Bevans told me Larry would love you."

At Anita's invitation Kathy sat beside her on a grey silk upholstered love seat before a multi-paned window that looked down upon the park. The normally splendid view was blurred now by sleet. Kathy was conscious of the elegance of the furnishings, both in this room and the expansive library beyond, where a man — his back to them — was hanging a wall of draperies.

With a polite smile Kathy listened to Anita's extravagant explanations for not spending the holidays with her son.

"You'll drive carefully, Kathy?" Anita's solicitude came across so phoney, Kathy thought. "And you'll start back early the morning after New Year's day to avoid the rush? The statistics on holiday accidents terrify me."

"We'll be in the car as soon as it's light enough to drive," Kathy promised. She, too, was fearful of holiday driving.

"I'll be desolate without my baby, but I'm so uptight seeing him like this." Anita bordered on melodrama, then managed a martyred smile. "I'll return from Palm Beach a better mother for the rest."

"I'm sure you'll enjoy the warmth and sun-shine." Kathy knew Anita Cantrell expected an outpouring of sympathy. *How could she run off to Palm Beach and leave that poor little boy alone with strangers at Christmas?*

Anita rose to her feet.

"Let me take you to Larry. Spend a little time getting acquainted with him, then the three of us will have dinner together. After that you'll be off to Salem."

"Fine." Kathy found it difficult to relax with Anita Cantrell. Sympathy welled in her for young Larry Ames. Surrounded by so much money, and he had so little.

"Larry has new ice-skates, and Neil Madison — who's in charge up there — assures me there are plenty of sleds. The children will have ice-skating parties and cook-outs on the pond. There'll be hayrides and sleigh-rides . . ." Anita exuded enthusiasm for the trip.

"It must be beautiful up there this time of year," Kathy said politely. But Larry couldn't see the beauty.

Anita glanced at her diamond-studded watch.

"We'll sit down to dinner at six-thirty. By eight you can be in the car with Larry. The traffic will be so light at that hour you should be in Salem by midnight. Larry is sure to sleep all the way. You can just transfer him to his bed. Neil Madison told me he would wait up to help you get settled in."

Kathy followed Anita up the carpeted stairs to

the second floor of the apartment. Down the hall Anita paused at a door.

"This is Larry's bedroom."

Kathy followed her into a mutely illuminated small boy's bedroom. Larry sat, small and forlorn, in an armchair by the window. He was listening to a game show on the colour TV across the room — which he could hear but could not see. A storybook little boy, Kathy thought tenderly. Curly honey-coloured hair atop a face of child-model handsomeness. Heavily lashed dark brown eyes that were wistful and unseeing now.

"Mrs Holmes?" Larry asked warily.

"No, darling," Anita corrected with an almost hysterical gaiety. "Don't you remember? Mrs Holmes left for her vacation right after lunch. You'll open your Christmas present from her up in the country. And here's Kathy, who's going to spend the holidays with you."

"Hello, Larry." Kathy's voice was gentle. She saw the small face tighten in alarm. Another face that he could not see. "We'll have a lot of fun together up in Salem," she promised.

"Did you bring me a Christmas present, too?" Larry asked. Not truly interested, Kathy thought. The present Larry wanted was his sight.

"Oh yes, I brought you a present," Kathy said with an air of conspiratorial conviviality. Thank goodness that she had thought of this.

"What is it?" Curiosity plus a faint imperiousness in his voice.

"You'll have to wait until Christmas Day,"

Kathy teased. "Tomorrow night we'll put it under the tree, and in the morning you'll open it."

"Last year I took him to see the Christmas tree at Rockefeller Plaza," Anita remembered with a sudden look of anguish on her face that Kathy found difficult to believe. "And the marvellous windows at Saks. Then the next day his father flew with him to St Thomas. He came back with a glorious tan."

"Why didn't Daddy come this year?" Larry was reproachful.

"Darling, I told you. He's stuck on some silly old assignment down in Rio." Annoyance lurked beneath the sweetness of Anita's reply. "Larry's father usually has him for the Christmas holidays, two weeks in the spring, and a month in the summer. He's always travelling. He's an engineer."

"I'm sure your father wanted to come," Kathy comforted. Such a lost look on Larry's face! He loved his father. He was so disappointed — and hurt — that he had not come. And now his mother was flying to Palm Beach. Leaving him with a total stranger. "I'll bet he's furious that he can t get away from his job."

"I'll leave you two to get acquainted." Anita seemed relieved that there had been no outburst from Larry. "I have some last-minute packing to do."

The afternoon dragged despite her efforts to amuse Larry. Only for a few moments — when he showed off the Christmas present from his father — did he come alive. *He was frightened.* Couldn't his mother understand that? Imprisoned by blindness. And now to go off with a stranger to a house four hours distant.

Kathy breathed a sigh of relief when Martha came to summon them to the dinner table. They sat down to a gourmet meal that she hardly tasted. She watched while Anita meticulously cut up Larry's food and fed him as though he was a toddler instead of a bright little six-year-old. And she suspected that this was a rare event. Instinctively she knew that he spent most of each day in the care of servants.

"Larry always has a straw with his milk. That makes it easier for him," Anita said. "Remember that, please."

"I'll remember," Kathy promised.

Chapter Two

In an expensive shearling jacket that Anita had bought for him only three weeks ago in the men's department at Saks, Randall slouched behind the wheel of his ancient Olds. He had opened the window about an inch because the heater was running. A road map, marked in red ink, lay beside him on the seat.

He had taken the spoils of his months with Anita — Italian suits she liked him to wear when they went out together to Elaine's or Lutece or Le Cirque, the St Laurent shirts, the Gucci shoes — to store with the publicity woman he had met at the Hamptons before Anita, and whom he had seen half a dozen times since. His rifle was wrapped in a blanket in the trunk. He had a hunting licence. He had no permit for the hand gun stashed away now in the car's glove compartment.

He pushed in the cigarette lighter, reached into his jacket pocket for a cigarette. Damn, the lighter wasn't working. Nothing in this car worked right any more. It had been old when he bought it four years ago, just before he left UCLA. The money had come from Maggie, his swinging English Lit professor.

Just last week he had gone into the store to talk to the salesman about the red Maserati in the window. Wow, that was a job! Anita knew how badly he wanted a great car. Damn her, she had all but promised him that Maserati. And now he sat here with a severance paycheque in his wallet and a pain in his head. *Rotten bitch.* She'd be sorry. Oh, would she be sorry for throwing him out on his ear!

Larry and that girl — her name was Kathy — ought to be arriving at the garage any minute now. Anita told her they were to be on the road by eight. It was a lousy night for driving. The corners of his sensuous mouth lifted. For him that was a plus. Not many people on the road tonight. He would find a spot where there was not another car insight.

At five to eight he spied Larry walking with Kathy. She was carrying Larry's suitcase in one hand, holding on to Larry with the other. Larry clutched a gaily wrapped Christmas package in his free arm.

Randall reached for the ignition. Warm the car so it wouldn't stall before he was ready to pull out. He leaned forward to watch the garage entrance. Racing the engine. His fingers tapped impatiently on the wheel as Larry and Kathy went into the garage.

A few moments later a Honda pulled out. He stiffened to attention. No. A man sat behind the wheel. They'd probably have to bring the car from upstairs. It had been sitting in the garage since early afternoon. It might take a few minutes.

Then a grey Dodge Spirit rolled out the garage

door, crossed the pavement, and turned into the street. Churning with fresh rage he squinted through the vision-impairing sleet. That was the car. Larry sat beside the girl at the wheel. Why hadn't she put the kid on the back seat to sleep, the way Anita told her?

The sleet made it necessary to drive slowly. No sweat to stay directly behind the grey Dodge. She would cut through the park, drive west and onto the Henry Hudson highway. He'd heard Anita and her discussing the route.

Randall leaned forward to flip on the radio as they waited for the red light to change at the corner of Fifth Avenue. He winced at the sounds of 'Key Largo' — he didn't want to think about Florida — and switched to another station.

The light changed. Hell, was the car going to stall? He swore under his breath as the car behind him honked raucously. He pushed the accelerator to the floor. The car bolted ahead. In moments he had caught up with the grey Dodge.

She was headed up the Henry Hudson, into the Saw Mill. She would cut off onto the Taconic, the way Anita told her, and then head onto Route 295 and 22. Long stretches of deserted road along the way, he surmised in satisfaction. All he needed was a few minutes like that. And it would be all over. Anita would be paid off in full.

He was whistling as he followed the grey Dodge into the park. Anita Cantrell would be forever sorry for the way she had treated him.

Chapter Three

Kathy's eyes left the road for a second as she pulled up before the stop sign that momentarily blocked their way onto the Henry Hudson highway.

"Are you warm enough, Larry?" she asked solicitously.

"Yes," Larry said in the scared little voice with which he had answered all of Kathy's questions since they'd left the apartment. Poor baby, he was so young to be shipped off alone with a stranger, she thought again.

"If you get cold, you tell me," Kathy encouraged. "We have a blanket back there on the rear seat."

Larry had not wanted to be put to sleep alone on the back seat. He had asked to be allowed to sit up front with her. The pillow was wedged against the door so that if he began to droop in sleep, his head would have a comfortable resting place.

"Let me be sure the door is locked." Kathy reached across Larry to check. Knowing she had locked the door but needing reassurance. And his seat belt was in place.

Traffic was not as light as Kathy had anticipated. Seeming heavier because of the necessity to drive slowly, she realised. Some Christmas office parties had run late, she guessed — worrying about drunken drivers.

She was relieved when they began to lose drivers at every exit. By the time they passed the first toll gate, only a trickle remained on the highway. And Larry showed no signs of going to sleep.

"Would you like some music, Larry?" Kathy asked cajolingly. Thus far, her efforts at conversation had been ineffective.

"OK." The same small, impersonal voice. What could she do to make him feel less alone, she asked herself with frustrating helplessness.

She fiddled with the radio dial until she found a recorded programme that filled the car with Christmas cheer. Wistfully — unwarily — she wished for a moment that she had flown to Texas to be with Robin and her family. Christmas was not a time to be alone among strangers. She reached out to fondle Larry's hand for a moment. Did his mother believe he was insensitive to the season?

By the time they arrived at the Taconic highway, Larry had fallen asleep. A sybaritic warmth permeated the car, providing a sense of security. Kathy lowered the music to a whisper. Yet she was uneasy on the dark, empty road. Shadows on either side lent an ominous aura to the night.

The sleet had changed to snow. Large flakes were falling with determined rapidity, lending an eerie brightness to the road now. No real problem, she soothed herself. By the time there was a troublesome build-up of snow on the road, they would be up in Salem.

She glanced at Larry. He was still asleep. He would probably sleep all the way up, as Anita Cantrell had predicted. Now the Taconic was all but deserted. Trees rose austerely tall into the darkness on either side of the road. She was comforted by the presence now of a car behind them. Someone like her, too cautious to speed in these treacherous driving conditions.

Kathy was glad that the other car remained behind them while occasional cars hurried past, splashing slush across her windscreen. If this kept up, she'd have to stop along the road to clean off the windscreen. The wipers were not coping.

Far up the Taconic Kathy began a slow, upward climb. It was a long, steep incline. She shifted into low gear. Frowning in annoyance as lights behind glared upon the windscreen. What was the matter with that stupid driver? Didn't he realise he was blinding her? Why was he tailgating?

All at once her heart began to pound. She checked again to make sure the doors were locked — remembering the increasing incidents of carjacking. At moments like this how reassuring it would be to have mobile phone.

The other car remained terrifyingly close. The lights distracting. Not a car-jacker, she tried to reassure herself. She wasn't being bumped. But how could he be so discourteous? She put her foot down to the floor in an impatience to pick up speed, though the incline was too steep to make real progress.

The driver behind stepped on his accelerator. His lights remained harsh on Kathy's windscreen. What was the matter with him? Was he drunk?

Suddenly the other car was no longer tailgating. He was pulling up beside her. Parallel to her. Her eyes shot in alarm to the window of the other car. It was too dark to see the lunatic behind the wheel.

Fear inundated her. *What did he want?* The doors were all locked, she remembered with an effort to reassure herself. He couldn't get into the car. Anxiously her eyes settled on Larry. He was still asleep.

She slowed down, hoping to drop behind the other driver. He lowered his own speed to remain parallel with her. So close now the cars were almost scraping. Her eyes grazed the area ahead. In a few moments they would be at the crest of the hill. She inspected the landscape. The land levelled off at her left. From the top there must be a deadly drop.

He meant to push them over at the top. That was what he wanted to do, wasn't it? Why?

For a split-second Kathy debated. Visualising that terrifying drop from the top. With all her strength she swerved off the road. Pushing through tangled clumps of bushes till the car came to a wrenching stop — in collision with tall, thick trees that grew beyond the bushes.

Larry wasn't asleep now. The silence of the

night was shattered by his frightened screams.

Randall jammed to a stop on the road. He had not planned it this way, but it would do. An empty dark road far from traffic. It would be hours — maybe days — before the kid and the girl were found. Why did the kid keep screaming that way? It made his headache worse.

He reached into the glove compartment for the .32. Suddenly he saw the blinding headlights of a truck that rolled over the hill. Damn! Why now? Get out of here! Quick!

He switched on the ignition again, pumped the gas into action. The car bolted ahead, whizzed past the truck. In his rear-view mirror he saw the truck pull to a stop by the side of the road. They had heard the dumb kid screaming.

"Larry, it's all right. Darling, it's all right," Kathy soothed, fumbling with his seat belt. "We just hit a tree."

She pulled Larry to her with masked anxiety, running her hands over the small body, crooning reassurances. The screaming reduced to frightened sobs now.

"Anybody hurt down there?" a rugged male voice called out, and Kathy heard footsteps crackling over frozen twigs.

"I don't think so," Kathy said shakily. "We smashed into a tree trunk."

She flinched as a burst of light flooded the car. A stocky man in a red and black chequered jacket

peered solicitously at them. A small, wiry man hovered behind him.

"You skid off the road?" the one at the rear asked matter-of-factly. "Some patches of ice here and there."

"Somebody pushed us off the road," Kathy said with perilously held calm while the man in the chequered jacket reached to bring Larry out of the car. Larry tensed, fumbled for Kathy's hand.

"Come on, little fellow. Let me help you outta here," he encouraged.

"It's all right, Larry," Kathy soothed. Squeezing one small hand encouragingly for a moment. "These men are helping us."

"I got one about your size at home," the man chuckled as he lifted Larry from the car. "Your kid?"

"We're very good friends," Kathy said while she slid out on the same side. "I'm taking Larry into the country for the holidays." In the spill of the flashlight she mimed the message that Larry was blind. She felt their compassion.

"What do you mean, somebody pushed you off the road?" the smaller man asked curiously while the two of them moved about to inspect the front of the car.

"It was crazy." Kathy frowned, recoiling from the memory of those moments. "First he was tailgating. I was terrified he was a car-jacker. Then he pulled up to drive along side us. Inches away. When I slowed down, he slowed down. When I picked up speed, he did the same. Then we were scraping sides. I was afraid of going over at the top, with that sharp drop." She was suddenly ice-cold, but not from the weather. "I figured the only thing to do was to swerve off the road."

"That black car we saw tearing away so fast?" The man in the chequered jacket straightened up. "You get a look at him?"

"No. It was too dark," Kathy told him.

"This time of year you always run into creeps like that," the other man said with distaste. "They get all tanked up at some office party, and somebody on the road almost gets killed. You're lucky it's no worse."

"You've got a cracked headlight and some dents," the stocky man reported. "I don't think there's any real damage. You want us to get the car up onto the road and check it out for you?"

"Oh yes, please." Kathy was grateful for their help.

Guiding Larry, who was silent and sombre-faced now, Kathy made her way up onto the road while the two men focused on the best way to bring the car up. Snow fell steadily about them. Kathy's eyes swept up and down the road. Not another car was in sight. How fortunate for Larry and her that the truck showed up at just that moment. She would have been terrified alone with Larry and the car down there.

In a few minutes the men had the car on the road and were checking it out. Apparently it was in good running order.

"That right headlight's cracked, but the bulb's still working," the man in the chequered jacket reported with an air of satisfaction. "How do you like that? Somebody's watching over you tonight. You'll get to where you're going with no trouble."

"Thank you so much." Kathy smiled in relief and gratitude. She lifted Larry into the car again and reached to fasten the seat belt. "I never would have got the car back on the road without you."

"Here, Larry." The smaller man reached to put a package of sweets into Larry's hand. "Something to keep you busy while you're riding."

"Thank you," Larry said uncertainly, but already he was fumbling in the package to pull forth one of the small sweets.

"There's a diner just down the road. Go in and have some coffee," the taller man urged. "It's just off the road, but it's easy to get off and on again."

"Yeah, you had a lousy experience," the other man reinforced. "Go in for coffee and relax."

"Thank you, I will." Now Kathy was trembling. All at once she was visualising what might have happened to them. *But it hadn't.* "Larry, would you like some hot chocolate?" she asked coaxingly.

"OK." But now there was something besides resignation in Larry's voice. Kathy and he had been through an adventure together. She sensed he felt a new closeness to her.

Chapter Four

Despite the draughts that infiltrated the car Randall was sweating. Then he spied the diner just off the road. Go in and have some coffee. Wait a while. Maybe the car wasn't in bad shape. They might be back on the road. She had ploughed into some trees, scared Larry. That was probably all that happened. He hadn't expected her to be so sharp. *Next time he'd be ready for her.*

He swung off the road and parked before the diner. A popular joint, he guessed, viewing the line-up of cars. He was hungry, he realised as he strode up the steps and into the brightly lit diner. He walked to a booth and sat down, ran a finger across the steamed-over window.

A pretty young waitress came over to take his order and promptly returned with a mug of strong black coffee. The way his head was pounding he needed coffee. Seeing the truck come over the hill that way had catapulted him into ugly recall.

How old had he been? Just eight, he remembered. His face etched in oft-repeated rage. His eyes darkened. They were living out in Pennsylvania then. . . .

"Hey, Randall go get the ball," the kid across the road jeered as he grabbed away the brand new football. Four years older than he and a bully. "Go get it!" He tossed Randall's football, a birthday present

34

from his parents, into the road.

"I'll kill you!" Randall screeched. He darted into the road without looking. After the prized football.

"Randall!" his mother screamed. Too late. "Oh, my God, Randall!"

The truck had borne down upon him, shattering bones, fracturing his skull. Keeping him in the hospital for long, painful weeks. But he had been something of a hero when he returned to school.

He never told anybody about the terrible headaches. Not even his mother. He was afraid he would be sent back to the hospital. For a long time he had awakened screaming in the middle of the night. Feeling that truck bearing down on him again.

The waitress brought his platter of ham, eggs, and French fries. She re-filled his coffee mug. As though he had pushed the proper button, he was again the super-confident, womanising Randall, flirting with the sexy little waitress.

He was glad for once that his ancient car was nondescript, unostentatious. All the truck driver would remember was that an old model black car shot up the hill. They couldn't have got his licence number. He was home free.

Even if he had lost the girl for the night, it would be easy enough to pick her up again in Salem. He'd look for a motel near town, check in for the night. No real rush. He had nine days to kill.

Chapter Five

Kathy drove slowly north on the Taconic highway. It was clear that up here the snow had begun to fall much earlier than in Manhattan. She suspected the build-up of snow on the road was at least three inches already. Despite the fact that she was progressing at no more than thirty miles an hour, at intervals she felt the ice beneath the white blanket of snow. Twice the car skidded.

The gritters ought to be out on the road soon. She would welcome their presence. Where was the diner the truckers had mentioned? She was tired. Coffee would go well about now. She refused to recognise that over half the trip to Salem lay ahead.

There was the diner. Relief welled in her. She slowed down at the approach to the turn-off to the diner, turned off the road and pulled to a stop in the parking area.

"We'll go in here and have hot chocolate," she told Larry with an air of conviviality. He had been so frightened when they crashed into that tree trunk. "There's a nice diner here." She reached to unhook his seat belt.

Kathy lifted Larry from the car. Hand in hand they walked to the diner.

"Four steps up, Larry," she said cautiously, and

36

together they mounted the stairs.

Kathy relished the rush of warmth that greeted them as she pulled the door open. A medley of pleasing aromas enveloped them. Coffee. Bacon sizzling on a grill. Spaghetti sauce simmering.

Kathy's eyes swept the booths. All full, she noted in disappointment. Larry would feel more at ease in the privacy afforded by a booth. No, the one directly behind the cashier was empty.

With a smile, Larry's hand tucked in hers, she moved towards what she believed was an empty booth, then paused self-consciously. In the far corner of the booth meant for four, sat a young man engrossed in a road map. He wore a shearling jacket that was a duplicate of one that was Clint's pride and joy. Ridiculously expensive.

"Excuse me," she apologised. "I thought this booth was empty."

She prodded Larry to the counter. They settled themselves on stools besides a middle-aged couple arguing good-humouredly about his sense of direction. The waitress came over with a smile.

"Larry, would you like a jam doughnut with your hot chocolate?" Kathy asked invitingly. Normally she would not have encouraged this indulgence in sweets, but he had eaten so little at dinner, despite his mother's repeated coaxing. Anita Cantrell, Kathy surmised, was a spasmodic and neurotically frantic mother. "They look delicious." The woman beside her grinned and held up a jam-rich half of the doughnut which had prompted Kathy's enquiry.

"OK," Larry agreed.

The woman beside them launched into a lively discussion about the weather. Kathy saw the compassion in her eyes as she became aware of Larry's blindness. Kathy had deliberately suggested the doughnut because Larry could cope with this without help.

When Larry's doughnut and hot chocolate were placed before him, Kathy brought his hand to the doughnut so that he could pick it up on his own. When the doughnut was demolished, clearly with pleasure, she put the spoon in one hand and led the other to the mug.

"Drink it with the spoon," she said. "It's hot." Let Larry learn a little independence. Couldn't his mother understand how important this was?

"I don't know what it is with Joe," the woman beside Kathy said with mock impatience while Kathy signalled the waitress to re-fill her coffee mug. "If there's a wrong way to go, that's where we head. Last time we tried to get onto Route 22, we landed sixty-five miles out of our way. Even on skis he loses his way." She laughed high-spiritedly. "Here we are pushing fifty and just learning to ski. I tell you, it's great."

"I'm headed for Route 22," Kathy told her. "We turn off the Taconic onto 295 and bear east to 22. Why don't you follow me? I'm going straight up 22 to Salem."

"Honey, that'll be wonderful," the woman said appreciatively. "Joe, you stick to their car, you hear? Once we're on 22, we're OK." The woman turned back to Kathy. "We know the turn-off there at the right that'll take us to Bennington."

They lingered briefly in the diner, then the four of them headed for their respective cars. Joe and his wife were in a red Fiat, skis atop. Driving back onto the highway Kathy checked the rear view mirror to be sure the couple was behind. It was reassuring to have them following the Dodge. Not tailgating the way that drunk had been, but close enough to make her feel comfortable.

Larry remained awake until they were nearing the end of the eleven mile stretch on Route 295. The temperature was dropping, but Kathy was reluctant to turn up the heat. With the car warm she might become drowsy. She mustn't take a chance on losing control of the car. She shivered, recalling the near-disaster on the Taconic highway.

At the turn-off onto 22 she pulled to a stop, reached into the back for a blanket, and tucked it around Larry.

Joe drew up beside her.

"That's 22, right?"

"Yes. But follow me anyway," she encouraged with a sudden need for their continued presence. "All right?"

"Sure," he agreed. "All the way up to the Bennington turn-off."

Few cars were driving north tonight. Just the Dodge, the red Fiat, and a car behind the Fiat. The other car carried skis atop, also. Everybody had skis on their cars up this way. Even that drunken driver who had pushed them off the road, she remembered now.

Kathy drove slowly. Nobody was making any real time with the roads icing up beneath the snow. When they arrived at the turn-off to Bennington, she pulled off to the side of the road, rolled down the window on Larry's side. The red Fiat came to a stop beside the Dodge.

For a few moments Kathy and the couple exchanged convivial conversation. Then the Fiat followed the turnoff at the right. Almost simultaneously a huge trailer truck swung out of the turn-off to follow behind Kathy as she headed north on 22. Cutting off the car that had been following in their wake earlier.

She was happy for the presence of the trailer truck behind her. Remembering the rescue efforts of the earlier truck. Suddenly she tensed. The trailer truck driver was signalling that he was going to pass her.

Kathy's eyes clung to the truck as the driver positioned himself ahead of her. She knew the driver had her image in his rear view mirror. Her lights would cause him no problem, she reminded herself subconsciously. The car at her rear was close, but not tailgating.

Half a mile up — on impulse — she signalled that she was going to pass the trailer truck. She drove with uncharacteristic speed to keep the truck behind her, glad to realise that he remained on Route 22. There was something comforting about the presence of the trailer truck.

She glanced at her watch as she read the sign that said 'Salem, 1 Mile'. The trailer truck still behind her. It was well past 1 A.M. already. She felt guilty about arriving at the house so late. But Mr Madison had told Anita Cantrell that he would wait up for them.

She drove past the sign that proudly stated that Salem was founded in 1764, past rows of modest houses that led into town. She read the plaques that commemorated battles of the American Revolution. Occasionally she spied a lighted window. Festive Christmas trees were in front of most houses. Their windows outlined with Christmas lights. Here was holiday spirit despite the hour.

In town, green and red lights were strung in rows across Main Street. Windows of the shops were decorated for the holiday season. Now she watched carefully for the street where she was to turn off. There.

She drove past several blocks of darkened houses. The houses became sparse as she moved further away from Main Street. The mountains in the distance were austere and white-capped. Trees outlined with snow. Somewhere in the distance a dog howled.

She drove past seemingly endless fields, then spied the silo on the left that told her the house would be on the right twenty feet beyond, per Anita Cantrell's direction. She slowed down, pleased that Neil Madison had lit the lamppost at the head of the driveway to guide her up to the house.

The big white house was set back at least a hundred feet from the road. Two storied, flanked by a huge annex which would contain the classrooms, dormitory and student dining hall. She swung into the driveway and was startled by a sudden clamorous squawking. A smile of recognition lit her face. Geese. The best of house sentinels.

She braked as a rabbit darted across the driveway, momentarily blinded by the headlights. Then he was scampering away into the shadows.

She drew to a stop before the house. All at once floodlights bathed the outdoors in an eerie brightness. The massive front door swung wide. A tall, slim man with sandy hair and casual good looks — clad only in slacks and a brilliant red pullover despite the cold — strode across the small porch and down the steps. Neil Madison. She had not expected him to be so young. Probably only two or three years older than herself.

"King, Sandy, shut up!" he good-humouredly reproached the noisy geese in a pen to the right. His voice was deep and mellow. "How are the roads?" he asked. "Did you have any trouble?"

"It was getting rough. I hope the gritters get out soon." She said nothing about the drunken driver that had so terrified her. "There're bad patches of ice under the snow." She leaned forward to release Larry's seat belt and to unlock the door.

"Let me take him." Neil opened the door. "I'll put your car in the barn later. It's a tricky manoeuvre."

"Aren't you freezing that way?" She hunched her shoulders as she stepped out into the near-zero night.

"We'll be in the house in a minute." What a pleasant, relaxed man, Kathy thought. "Let me take Larry." Gently he scooped Larry into his arms. "I'll put up coffee while you get him into bed. You two will have Laura Hanley's room and the little sitting room that adjoins it. She's in Europe for the holidays." He grinned wistfully. "Oh, there's deep dish apple pie to go with coffee. Mrs McArdle, who comes in from the village to do the cooking — she's in residence over the holidays — made the pie to welcome you."

"That sounds great," Kathy approved.

With Larry cradled in his arms, Neil led the way into the house. The living room was large, with a huge fieldstone-faced fireplace and a beamed ceiling. The room was pleasantly furnished with Early American reproductions. The slipcovers and drapes in bright, cheery patterns. An enormous log burned in the grate, where the ashes beneath indicated that this was a regular practice.

Oh yes, Kathy told herself, she was glad she had agreed to come up here with Larry. It would be a lovely, brief escape from the outside world. The terror of those moments on the hill — when death seemed to be breathing down their necks — could be locked away in a crevice of her mind. That was behind them now.

Chapter Six

Randall saw the 'Vacancy' sign at a motel by the road. This was close enough to town. Check in. He pulled up before the sign that said 'Office' and emerged from the car. He peered inside the office. One low-wattage lamp glowed within. The door was locked. Then he spied a scrawled memo that instructed callers to buzz for service.

In moments a man in a bathrobe emerged from the rear. He came to open the door, greeted Randall with a welcoming smile. Business must be slow here, Randall surmised.

"Yes sir, we got a vacancy," he said in reply to Randall's inquiry. He reached for a registration card. "You up for the skiing? Should be great by tomorrow."

"I plan to do some skiing," Randall conceded casually. From habit he had brought along skis. Also, it made him look part of the scenery. He had not ski'd since Aspen, a year ago. "And I mean to do some hunting."

"You expect to stay for a while?"

"Anywhere from one day to nine. It depends." He busied himself with the registration card. Giving a phoney name. Any trouble later he could always say the car had been stolen. He kept it parked on Manhattan streets. Thousands of cars got stolen every year. Sometimes people didn't notice for days. But there wouldn't be any trouble.

The motel manager gave him a key.

"Unit eight, right at the curve," he pointed. The motel units were built in a u-shape. "Have a good night."

Randall brought his flight bag from the back of the car, sauntered into the modest unit. The bedspread was an overly-washed orange chenille. The furniture was run-of-the-mill budget motel style. He unpacked his Calvin Klein toiletries and lined them up atop the dresser. He remembered his room in Anita Cantrell's penthouse duplex and grimaced in distaste. But this would do until the job was done.

He moved to the window to snap the venetian blinds tight, but paused first to gaze at the darkly outlined mountains that rose in the distance. He remembered the girl in Aspen, who had a thing about flying over the mountains. The Andes, the Alps, the Rockies. Half a dozen times a year she made the trip, just for the sense of power flying over a mountain gave her. He could understand that. He felt the same way.

If Anita hadn't got scared of her mother, he would have had the whole deal for himself. The great apartment in New York. The beach house at East Hampton. The ski lodge up in Stowe. Money to buy everything he wanted. Including that red Maserati.

Let Anita go down to Palm Beach and work things out with her mother. *It wouldn't mean a*

46

thing. With Larry dead the trust fund from his grandfather's estate would go to some musty old museum. That was in the will.

Anita would pay for what she did to him. She led him to the top of the mountain, then she booted him down to the bottom. He'd never forget the way she looked at him when he said he'd marry her. Like he was dirt. She should have grabbed at the chance to marry him! She was three months from forty. He was twenty-four.

He clicked the blinds shut and spun away from the windows. That same dull pain that plagued him earlier pressed against his head. His eyes rested on a local farm implements company calendar — depicting a pair of deer by a winter-iced stream — that hung over the dresser. He reached for a pen from his jacket pocket, walked to the calendar, and crossed off December 23rd.

Eight days to kill.

Chapter Seven

Comfortably seated in a Boston rocker before the Franklin stove in the huge square country kitchen of the main house, Kathy listened as Neil talked.

"It does something beautiful for me," Neil was summing up, an earnest glow about him, "to see what we're able to do for these kids. Fifty years ago they would have been lost. Written off as misfits."

"They're bright children with real futures ahead of them because — thank God — we've discovered how to teach them to learn," Kathy said, relishing Neil's sentiment — which echoed her own. Clint had thought only of the exorbitant fees he could charge once he had his doctorate.

"Some learning disabled kids have to hold a book straight up before they can see it. Sometimes they see letters backwards. Some have tactile problems. Some have to hear and repeat. But Kathy, we know how to cope." All at once Neil seemed embarrassed at displaying such intensity of emotion. He rose to his feet. "More coffee?"

"All right." A hint of conspiratorial laughter in her voice. How many times had Neil re-filled their mugs since they sat down before the Franklin stove?

"My first investment when I get back to New

York," Neil said with a grin, "will be a coffee grinder. How can I live without freshly ground coffee after being spoiled up here this way?"

"Do you know, it's almost 3 A.M.!" Kathy's eyes focused with disbelief on the clock that hung on the wall to her left. "We've been talking for almost two hours!"

"I'm sorry I've kept you up," he apologised, bringing the percolator to re-fill her mug. "I lost track of time."

"I've loved hearing about your work here." There was something disconcerting and yet exhilarating about the way his eyes lingered on her as he talked.

Why did she feel this pull towards Neil? Was she reacting to the break-up with Clint? No. This was something new. She'd been drawn to Clint because she'd been hurting and lonely. This was different.

"Drink up and go to bed," Neil ordered. He, too, was all at once self-conscious. "But don't expect anybody to be up early. Not even Mrs McArdle shows up in the kitchen before eight. She feeds us practically on demand," he explained humorously. "The children are living here in the house with us instead of in the dorm." Now his eyes were sombre. "To give them a feeling of being home for the holiday." Children stranded far from home at a most special time of year.

Kathy knew that her compassion for the five pupils — and for Larry — was duplicated in Neil.

49

Each aware of the other's feelings, they left the kitchen. Neil walked her upstairs to the tiny suite she shared with Larry.

"Sleep well," he said gently, pausing at the door.

"I will," she assured him. "Like the dead."

Instantly a coldness closed in about her. She was trembling. Larry and she would be dead if she had not swerved away from the road at just that moment. *That stupid drunk.*

Kathy had put Larry to bed in the bedroom. She would sleep on the made-up studio couch in the tiny sitting room. Now she went into the bedroom to make sure he was covered. The heat was low for the night.

Poor baby. How lost he must feel in that newly dark world of his. Anger welled in Kathy that neither parent had made the effort to be with their son at Christmas.

In a phone booth at the Rio airport David Ames fed a handful of coins into the indicated slot and waited impatiently to be connected. This was his second try. Moments ago the international operator had told him there was no reply at the other end. Where would Larry be except at home? But then Anita was always running off somewhere, he remembered and was uneasy. Still, she'd said nothing about going away when he called to say he couldn't be in New York for Christmas Eve.

"Hello . . ." he spoke again to the operator.

He managed a polite reply to her repeat of what the previous operator had told him. No one answered the phone in Anita's apartment. Damn, he wanted to tell Larry that he couldn't be there for Christmas, but he'd be back in New York right after. He felt a surge of anguish as he remembered the hurt in Larry's voice when he explained he couldn't be home for Christmas.

Where the hell *was* Larry?

Kathy fell asleep minutes after she slid beneath the blankets. She came awake six hours later. She heard the heat clanking in the old-fashioned radiators beneath the windows. The room was deliciously warm.

Then she became aware of pleasant aromas close by. Fresh bread baking in the oven, she thought with delight. Her mind catapulted into childhood recall. When she was little, she had been allowed to help knead the dough on those special occasions when Mom baked bread. Always on Christmas morning.

Brilliant sunlight filtered around the side of the shades. On impulse she thrust aside the blankets, crossed to a window and pulled the shade up to stare outdoors. Her mouth parted in a spontaneous smile at the sight of the glorious landscape of snow and mountain and sky. What a joyous day! So different from last night.

Truantly her mind zoomed in again on those panic-brushed minutes on the Taconic. Forget it, she exhorted herself. That was a freakish near-accident. Something like that happened once in a lifetime.

She pulled on her robe, gathered together toiletries, and headed for the bathroom. She heard voices in the kitchen. Mrs McArdle and Neil. He had said they would be having their meals in the kitchen or the family dining room off the kitchen rather than in the dining hall.

As she dressed, Kathy listened to the sounds from the other part of the house. Neil had just put up the Christmas tree, she gathered. This evening the tree would be decorated. In warm grey flannel slacks and a brilliant blue turtleneck sweater, she looked in on Larry again. He still slept soundly.

Kathy moved out into the hall. An auburn-haired, freckle-faced boy of about nine charged into view.

"Hi," he called out exuberantly with only fleeting curiosity about her presence. "I'm gonna help Neil bring in the tree!"

Chuckling at his impetuosity Kathy followed him down the stairs at a slower gait. She turned into the kitchen, intrigued by the aromas that wafted from the room. A small, rotund, fiftyish woman with her hair pulled back in a careless bun — comfortably garbed in slacks and a man's green corduroy shirt — hovered before the ultra-modern double oven. She had pulled one door down to inspect the contents. Mrs McArdle, Kathy was sure.

"Bread's ready," Mrs McArdle announced

with satisfaction while the little boy craned for a view. "Jamie, watch you don't get burnt. That's no way to spend Christmas. I won't put the other two breads in until I hear the other kids are awake." A pair of loaf pans sat on the bar that divided the room. The dough in each had risen to awesome heights.

"Good-morning," Kathy said warmly.

At the same moment Neil appeared in the doorway with a log in tow. His face brightened at the sight of her.

"Hi, sleep well?"

"Marvellously."

"Mrs McArdle, this is Kathy Anderson," Neil introduced them. Mrs McArdle beamed in welcome. "Kathy and Larry are staying with us till New Year's." Mrs McArdle knew that, of course. "And Kathy, this is Jamie."

"Hi, Jamie." Kathy's smile was dazzling. She felt wonderful this morning. "That apple pie last night was luscious, Mrs McArdle." She turned again to Jamie. "I'll bet everything Mrs McArdle bakes is great."

"Oh, sure." He grinned in anticipation. "Wait till you eat her chocolate chip cookies."

"You three sit down at the table here, and I'll throw on the ham and eggs to go with that bread," Mrs McArdle said. "The coffee's ready. Neil, you pour for Kathy and yourself. Jamie, get yourself a glass of milk from the refrigerator."

"OK." Jamie headed for the refrigerator. The involvement of Jamie was calculated to make him

53

feel he was home, Kathy surmised. "Can I go look at the Christmas tree after breakfast?"

"Jamie, you'll be looking at it till New Year's," Neil chided good-humouredly. "Wait till we decorate it tonight. It looks forlorn sitting in there naked that way."

"Last year I was home for Christmas." All at once Jamie's voice was accusing. His eyes rebellious. "That was before the divorce."

"Hey, you know what we'll do after breakfast?" Neil said quickly. "We'll go up to the pond and ice-skate. Kathy, did you know we have a two acre pond up there behind the house?" His eyes pleaded with her to follow his lead.

"No, I didn't." She made a point of sounding impressed. "Larry will love that."

"Why's he here?" Jamie demanded. "Wouldn't his school keep him?"

Kathy, Neil and Jamie lingered at the large round table at one side of the room. Jamie talked compulsively about his family. His mother was in Bermuda. "She hates the winter." His father was at Chamonix. "He loves to ski."

Kathy excused herself to check on Larry, though she knew that she would hear if he called to her. Larry was still asleep. No memories of last night's horror disturbed him. But Larry didn't know how close they had been to death.

Kathy returned to the table. The other children wandered downstairs. Nine-year-old Andrew and the three girls — all of them ten — regarded Kathy with friendly curiosity, then settled down

54

at the table with an air of resignation that disturbed Kathy.

This was Christmas. The children should be bubbling over with expectancy. She must buy some small gift for each of them, she decided, despite the state of her finances. Jamie and Andrew, and Livvy, Jean and Ellen. When could she shop, she asked herself uneasily. Tonight was Christmas Eve.

"Kathy?" Larry's voice, faintly shrill with alarm at waking alone in a strange room, filtered downstairs. "Kathy?"

"I'm coming, Larry!"

Hastily Kathy rose to her feet and hurried from the kitchen. Guilty now that she had not remained upstairs until he had awakened.

Chapter Eight

Randall poised at the crest of the slope, preparing to streak down with the effortless grace he demanded of himself. The girl — Chris something or other — watched him from below with the familiar admiration. He had been irritated at first when she arrived on the slopes minutes before he appeared. He relished solitude on the side of a mountain. It provided him with a gratifying sense of power. But this girl might be useful.

"Watch this, Chris!" he called out arrogantly, and pushed off into swift descent. Plotting manoeuvres that would impress her.

Chris charged towards him as he arrived at the bottom.

"You're terrific!" She was wide-eyed in approval. "I've been coming here for four years, but I'll never be as good as you!" She was about nineteen and well-built. In ten years, Randall guessed cynically, she would be fading and fat.

"I've been skiing since I was four," he lied. "My folks used to take me to Switzerland every Christmas." His parents had never been on skis in their lives. His father's favourite exercise had been lifting a beer bottle to his mouth. He had learned to ski when he was twelve. The minister had taken him skiing as a reward for choir boy activities. "I ski'd with my mother and sisters at Aspen last

Christmas," he said with an air of pleased reminiscence. He hadn't seen any of them for four years. Not since he dropped out of UCLA. He had not even bothered to send a postcard. He didn't need them any more. "Come on, Chris, let's go somewhere for breakfast." The Randall Brooks charm was in full swing. "I'm starving."

"I oughta go home." Chris was ambivalent. But she would go with him for breakfast. And then to his motel room. So the morning would not be a total waste, he thought in rare high spirits. The hours on the slope had eased his headache.

He could survive with no sweat on four hours sleep a night, he told himself with pride. Larry and that nursemaid would probably sleep till noon after that long haul last night. Maybe he didn't pull off the job as planned, but he shook them up plenty. They didn't know what was going down.

He would head out for the school when Chris and he split. He had to size up the place. Map out a campaign. Like a general lining up a battle.

His smile was complacent. No doubt about the outcome of this battle. The kid didn't have a chance to survive this operation. They didn't even know war had been declared.

Randall remembered the attractive roadside restaurant that caught his eye en route to the slopes. Nothing pretentious, but pleasant. A large square log cabin with an enormous fireplace. Take Chris there, eat, roll a mile down the road to his motel, and into bed.

"I saw a great place not far away." He prodded Chris towards their cars.

"I've gotta be home by two," she warned. "I have to wash my hair before I go to the tavern to work. And it's a good distance away."

"You'll be home by two," he promised cheerfully. "Get in your car and follow me. You'll like this place."

"The Log Cabin," Chris guessed. Her eyes told him she read the routine loud and clear. "All the tourists like it."

"The Log Cabin," he confirmed. So she had labelled him a tourist. Great.

A table near the log-laden fireplace was vacated as they arrived. Randall noted the hunting licence pinned to the rear of the jackets of the three men who were leaving. Hunting season was in high gear, though deer were out of season.

He could move around the countryside with his hunting licence on display, rifle in hand, and no questions asked. When he picked off the kid — retreating before he could be caught — people would say, "What a tragic hunting accident!" They happened every year.

Chris was familiar with the Log Cabin. She told him to order the home fries with their ham and eggs.

"Sensational," she promised. Her eyes telling him she considered him sensational. She was hot as a pistol, he guessed with odd detachment.

Anita was hot. Nobody was as passionate as a rich broad pushing forty. Damn her for what she

58

did to him! But she'd get hers. She couldn't live the way she liked without being able to dip into the kid's trust fund. But the trust fund would go to that museum when the kid was dead.

He pretended to be listening to Chris' raunchy flow of town gossip. He was annoyed that he had come up in such a rush that he'd had no time to buy bullets for the rifle. But he always had a round for the .32 in the glove compartment of the car.

That looked like a great sporting goods store he saw in town this morning. Just inspecting the windows he knew that. No, his mind rejected — don't buy bullets there. In a store like that they remembered their customers. Ask the guy at the motel about somewhere outside of town. Sometimes the big stores at the shopping centres sold bullets. Sure they would, in hunting country like this.

Randall and Chris wasted little time over breakfast. Afterwards they headed for his motel. The girl was a cow, he thought as he hovered over her in bed. No class. Anita had class. Still, this was a relationship he would keep up until he left town. Which, he told himself with vindictive pleasure, might be any day. Maybe tomorrow.

Chris drove off in high spirits. But she wasn't as experienced as she pretended to be, Randall assessed. Not that she hadn't kicked up her heels for plenty before him. Now Randall stopped by the motel office to ask about a store where he could buy bullets for his hunting rifle. He listened

59

carefully to directions. Getting into the car he checked his watch. A few minutes to two.

The shopping centre was in the opposite direction from town. Before he went there, he had to go back to town and look up the school. He couldn't make a move until he knew the lay of the land. He wouldn't even have to ask directions, he congratulated himself. Anita had all but written a blueprint for him when she talked to the girl while he hung the drapes in the library. He should have walked out without hanging them, but he'd been afraid she might stop payment on his cheque. She was bitchy enough to do that.

Randall drove into town, swung off Main Street at the traffic light. The only light in town, he guessed contemptuously. Stay on this road. Anita told the girl — Kathy something or other — that the house would be on the right. There'd be a sign for sure.

One hundred acres went with the school. There would be outbuildings, he guessed. They would mask his presence about the grounds. He had to get a feel of the schedule the kids followed. So he'd know when to make his move.

If no opportunity presented itself fast, he promised himself, then he would make one. *Larry Ames was marked for death.*

Randall drove along the winding road. He was aware of the splendour of the scenery but unmoved by it. His eyes watched for the silo. He tensed when he spied it at the top of the incline. OK. Drive past. Turn around. Park down the road a few hundred feet.

'No Hunting' signs were fastened to trees along a long road frontage. A hundred acres was a good sized tract to people around here. He'd like to own about fifty thousand acres. Maybe down in South America, where you could hire help for peanuts. Maybe he'd take himself down there after he saw Anita do her number over the kid. That severance cheque would pay his airfare down there and provide eating money for a while.

He pulled into a driveway, turned around, drove back past the house. In the country stillness he could hear the sounds of children in the distance. Probably back at the house somewhere. Skating, he decided. Anita said there was a pond for skating. It would be frozen over now.

He parked at the side of a snow-covered field, debated a moment, then reached into the glove compartment for the .32 and ammunition. If he saw the kid alone, he'd be ready. He could pick him off with no sweat at fifty feet.

The gun stuck behind his belt, Randall left the car to cross the road. If anybody spied him, he was a tourist walking through the woods. He didn't realise this was private property. Nobody would know he carried a .32 beneath his shearling jacket.

A German Shepherd charged forward, barking vociferously. Randall ignored the dog and strode down the road. He moved into the woods at the area where the 'No Hunting' signs began to appear. That would be the beginning of school property.

He walked swiftly. With a sense of excitement. This was no different from tracking big game. You used your brains. That was the difference between man and animal. So in this instance he was stalking a little boy and a girl — who had no inkling they were being tracked. The girl probably thought some nut had tried to shove her off the road. Nobody knew the truth. Nobody would ever know.

The land alternated between wide swathes of woods and open fields. Sufficient woods to hide him when he needed this. About two hundred feet from the house he discovered a collapsing barn. The roof had long ago caved in, along with two sides. Off-limits to the kids for sure. It was a hazard. The brand new barn — a brilliant red addition — far to the other side of the house would be the one in use.

He gloated about the presence of the old barn. It would be a great cover for him. He could position himself behind an area of weather-beaten siding and have a clear view of the house. Stimulated by this awareness he moved to a more advantageous position. Frozen twigs snapping beneath his rubber-soled camping boots.

Then he stiffened in wariness. Geese were squawking like maniacs. Worse than a pack of beagles. He hadn't figured on this.

"Hold on, you characters!" A man's voice ricocheted through the crisp winter air. Randall saw him step from the rear of the house. He was pulling on a bulky plaid jacket. "I'll let you out in a minute."

The man strode towards the pen. The geese continuing to upbraid him noisily. He talked to them as he approached. Randall watched while he opened the pen. Silent now, the geese zoomed out. Their webbed feet skimmed inches above the snow as they cavorted in the joy of freedom, moving towards the wide expanse of land before the house.

"Neil!" a woman called from the back door. "You'd better tell the kids to get back here in a few minutes. I'm putting their lunch on the table."

"I'll go up and tell them," he called back.

Randall waited until the man was far up the slight incline that led to the pond before he moved from his position. The geese didn't hear him. At least, they paid no heed. OK, he decided. He'd come back here and stalk the kid at a time of day when the geese were out of the pen. When they were down in front of the house. It would be easy enough to see them from the road, then come up here.

Whistling softly to himself, he headed back for the car. Now he would drive over to the shopping centre and buy himself some bullets. He felt in the inside pocket of his jacket. His hunting licence was there. His licence to kill.

Chapter Nine

Kathy watched with a surge of tenderness as Neil
— on his haunches before Larry — talked to him
with infinite encouragement. Neil was magnificent with children.

"Of course you want to go riding with us in the
wagon," Neil cajoled. "You missed the skating
this morning, but you don't want to miss this.
You'll sit right beside me. Behind those sensational Shire horses. The biggest horses of all.
Almost six feet high. They'll carry us all around
the countryside, where everything smells just
wonderful."

"OK," Larry agreed after a moment's hesita-
tion. "I'll go with you." But Kathy saw a certain
wariness in the way he extended his hand to Neil.

"I'll run inside for your jacket," Kathy said
quickly.

In a few moments Kathy returned with Larry's
jacket, a scarf, gloves. Helping Larry into the
jacket she realised this would be her chance to
shop for presents for the other children. Neil said
they'd be out at least two hours. Mrs McArdle
had prepared a jug of hot chocolate to go along
with them.

Kathy stood at a window while the children
piled into the waiting wagon and wrapped blankets across their laps. Larry sat between Neil and

the farmer who was providing the ride. As the huge Shires trotted down the driveway, Kathy heard the children's voices raised exuberantly in song. It would be good for Larry to be out with the other children, she thought with pleasure.

In her plum down coat, over wool slacks and a hunter green ski sweater, Kathy paused at the kitchen door with Mrs McArdle for last minute instructions about reaching the shopping centre. Neil had brought her car out of the barn and left it in the driveway for her.

Settling herself behind the wheel she tried to thrust Neil from her mind. It was disconcerting, the way he kept infiltrating her thoughts. There was something reassuringly solid and substantial about Neil. He was warm and tender and bright. All at once she recognised the difference between Clint and Neil. Neil was a man. Clint had been an irresponsible boy. It wasn't a question of years but of growing up.

Kathy followed the road into town. She watched for the turn that would take her to the shopping centre. A few miles out of town she spied the attractive log cabin restaurant at the side of the road. A marvellous aroma. Driving past the log cabin she saw a tall Christmas tree beside the fireplace, where a blaze roared in the grate.

The shopping centre parking area was jammed with cars of last-minute shoppers. She had to wait for a couple to pull out before she could park. Sliding into the empty space, she catalogued mentally the children for whom she was to shop.

Jamie, whose father was at Chamonix and whose mother was in Bermuda. Andrew, whose family was in Belgium, where his father was on a government assignment. Livvy and Jean had said nothing about their parents' whereabouts, but their eyes had seemed mature beyond their years at this discussion. Ellie's father had committed suicide eight years ago. She couldn't remember him. Her mother was in a Boston hospital recovering from open-heart surgery. Darling Ellie, Kathy thought with gratitude, who was so motherly to Larry.

She left the car and hurried into the cozy warmth of the huge store. The check-out counters were lined up with purchase-laden customers. She pulled a trolley from the cluster at one side of the entrance and made her way to the toy section — tabulating the amount she could spend for toys. And she must buy some humorous gift for Neil and Mrs McArdle and the girl who came in to clean.

With gratifying swiftness she made her choices and headed through the cluttered aisles towards the check-out counter.

Chapter Ten

Randall strode away from the sporting goods section at one side of the store. The place was mobbed — with so many people buying hunting equipment — that nobody would remember him. Dozens of hunters must be out in the area this week.

He walked with hunched shoulders, tense from his determination to push this campaign through as early as possible. Not seeing the trolley that moved from the aisle at a right angle to him.

"I'm sorry!" a girl's voice gasped in apology as the trolley she pushed crashed into him as he took his place in line.

"That's all right." He was brusque. Not bothering to glance at her.

"Oh, you were on the Taconic last night —" Stiffening in shock Randall swung to face her. The girl with Larry. *How could she have seen him in that darkness?* "We saw you in the diner," she explained as she fell into line behind him. Relief surged through him. She hadn't seen him in the car.

"I went in there for dinner. You came in with a little boy." All at once he was exuding charm. What a break! Use this chance encounter. Everything was playing right into his hands. "Did you come up from New York?"

"Yes, I did." Now she seemed uneasy at having launched this conversation with a stranger. Move in quick before she cut out.

"I went to school on the Coast — UCLA — but I work in New York now," he fabricated. She wouldn't think this was a pick-up. People were informal out here. "For a ski shop. This is my vacation. Weren't the roads lousy last night?"

"I hate driving on snow," Kathy admitted, and frowned at the number of customers ahead of them in the line.

"This time of year we have to expect long lines," he said sympathetically. "I'm Rick Jamison." The name he had given at the motel. And to Chris.

"Kathy Anderson." She responded, as he had anticipated, to his considerable charm.

"Look, there's a sensational place down the road," he said as though on impulse. "Open fireplace. The best coffee in Washington County. I don't know a soul up here . . ." The 22-carat Randall Brooks charm was turned on high. "Take pity on me and talk to me over coffee for a while?"

She was startled.

"I think I know the place . . ." She was searching for a polite way to turn him down.

Move fast, Randall ordered himself. "Actually, I've been trying to get up the nerve to ask for some advice. I have to pick out a present for my kid sister. Her birthday is next week. I shipped out her Christmas present but didn't get around to the birthday deal." The inference was that his family lived in California. "I haven't the foggiest notion what a seventeen-year-old girl likes in the way of sweaters. I kept delaying to the last minute. Have coffee with me — I'll tell you about Donna — and you can give me some idea about colour and sizes and what to look for."

"All right," she capitulated. "We'll talk about it over coffee."

"Follow me in my car," he coaxed. She wouldn't recognise the car from last night. It had been too dark on the road. She had been too scared. "Or we can go in mine and I'll bring you back here."

"I'll follow you," she decided. It was an innocuous situation that way, he interpreted her thinking. She figured he wouldn't make a pass.

At this hour the restaurant was lightly populated. Randall chose the same table near the fire where he had sat with Chris. He was relieved that the friendly waitress made no remarks about his having been in the restaurant earlier.

"What brought you up here?" he asked with a show of friendly curiosity, and listened while she told him about her temporary job and about Larry's blindness.

"Poor little kid," he sympathised. "That's rough." It was lucky he had been standing on a ladder hanging those drapes, with his back to the sitting room, when she arrived yesterday afternoon. But he would have to be sure Larry never heard his voice. Larry would recognise him.

"My motel manager keeps carrying on about a terrific look-out point close to town," Randall picked up enthusiastically. "You get a view of Manchester, Bromley, and North Bennington. He said the roads are clear. No problem getting up there. Maybe you'd like to drive up with me tomorrow sometime. It's a spectacular view," he reiterated. "And if you like," he made it sound like a generous after-thought, "bring along the little boy. I know he can't see, but you can describe it to him. And the air is marvellous up there. Unbelievable." *He would arrange to meet them midway, then position himself along the route and pick off Larry from the woods.* A hunting accident, like you read about every year in the newspapers.

"Thanks. It sounds lovely. But we'll be busy with the children all Christmas Day," Kathy told him.

"Some other time," he offered casually. "I'll be up here a while. Possibly until New Year's Day." He reached for a pen from his jacket pocket and jotted down his motel name and phone number on the corner of a paper napkin. "Here . . ." He handed her the napkin. "Give me a buzz if you feel in the mood for a sensational view. And if you like, bring along the kid. I know you feel obligated to spend most of your time with him."

Kathy smiled. She appreciated his solicitude for the kid, he decided. That was the way to play the game.

"Thanks. I'll see how my schedule works out."

She tucked the napkin away in her purse.

The waitress arrived with their coffee. Randall leaned back in his chair while she served them. Subconsciously one hand felt for his jacket pocket, where he had stashed the bullets. One of them was for Larry. If Kathy saw him, she'd have to get one, too.

Chapter Eleven

Kathy moved quietly about the tiny sitting room of the suite she shared with Larry. One lamp lit against the evening darkness. Moonlight spilled over the snow, visible through the drapes Kathy had opened in order to enjoy the view. From the kitchen came the tantalising aromas of pies baking in the oven. Pumpkin, mincemeat, and pecan.

Like the other children Larry was napping after the long afternoon of outdoor air. The nap had been a firm order from Neil because they were taking the children to the candlelight service at the church after dinner.

"Kathy?" Larry's voice was faintly distrustful as he came awake in the strange room which he could not see.

"I'm here, Larry." She moved to the bedroom.

"What are you doing?"

"I'm trying to decide what to wear to dinner." Kathy glanced at the small travel clock on the dresser. The turkey was scheduled to come out of the oven at seven sharp. "We'll be eating soon. Are you hungry?"

"Yes," Larry said with conviction. "What are you going to wear?" he asked after a moment.

"I think I'll wear a long skirt that I particularly like," Kathy decided. "Remember how stained glass windows look? In churches?"

"Uhh-huhh," Larry said. Frowning in recall.

"Well, that's my skirt. And I have a bright blue silk top with long sleeves and a neckline cut like a V." Would Neil like the outfit? "The top is soft and silky."

"It sounds pretty," Larry said.

Kathy dressed, then helped Larry into his clothes. They could hear the sounds of the others gathering already in the dining room. They would have dinner, go to church services, and come home to trim the Christmas tree.

"We'll see Christmas Day in together," Neil had promised the children with an air of conspiracy. He would have flown to California to spend Christmas with his family, but he had agreed to stay here. It wasn't all philanthropic, she forced herself to acknowledge. This would be part of the research for his doctoral thesis. "Five minutes after midnight," Neil had stipulated, "I'll chase you all off to bed."

Hand in hand Kathy and Larry walked downstairs and into the dining room. Ellie and Livvy were helping Mrs McArdle set the table. Jean stayed by a window and watched a stray dog wander about the grounds.

"He won't hurt the geese, will he?" Jean was anxious.

"He'll get the worse of it if he tries." Mrs McArdle chuckled. "When King and Sandy peck, honey, you feel it!"

"Kathy, you look beautiful," Jamie said enthusiastically. She had told the children they could call her by her first name.

"Thank you, Jamie." She was aware, also, of admiration in Neil's eyes.

"Neil, what's a candlelight service?" Andrew was dubious about the pleasure involved. "Do you listen to the minister by candlelight?"

"Oh, the service includes lots of singing," Neil said.

"You'll hear Christmas carols and hymns by the choir, and then we'll all sing."

"Not me." Andrew giggled. "My mother always tells me to just open my mouth and pretend I'm singing. I'm tone deaf." All at once Andrew's small face grew sombre. He was remembering that this was Christmas Eve, and he was here in a house full of strangers. Kathy curbed her instinct to reach out to pull him to her in comfort.

They settled about the table, covered by a colourful holiday tablecloth. Christmas candles flanked the turkey, which Mrs McArdle had sliced in the kitchen with an electric knife and then put together again, knowing this would cause hilarity among the children.

In the midst of much laughter, as Neil served, two shots echoed in the distance. Kathy started. Her eyes swung to Neil in involuntary alarm.

"Somebody's bagging Christmas dinner," Neil said casually. Why had she reacted that way, she reproached herself. They were in the country. "There's some shooting up here for sport," Neil continued, "but more often than not the

74

local hunter is adding to the family larder. Money's not in huge supply in these parts. But nobody hunts on our hundred acres," Neil emphasised. "The game warden would have their heads."

"I hate guns." Kathy grimaced in distaste.

"I never hunt," Neil said quietly. "I could never bring myself to kill an animal unless there was a desperate need for food."

"When I was ten," Kathy said, cold with recall even all these years later, "a classmate who lived across the way from us accidentally killed his younger sister with a hunting rifle. He didn't know it was loaded."

Mrs McArdle brought in bowls of stuffing, vegetables, and home-made cranberry sauce. Neil launched into a series of reminiscences about the past weeks of school, presumably to amuse Kathy but actually to involve the children in the table conversation. At intervals shots rag out in the distance. Kathy flinched with each report.

"Larry, you're gonna like the candlelight service," Ellie said earnestly. "I like to close my eyes and listen." How canny she was, Kathy thought tenderly. How compassionate.

"Were you always blind?" Jamie asked matter-of-factly, and Kathy tensed.

"No." There was an edge of defiance in Larry's voice. "I used to see. Before . . ."

"Before what?" Jamie pursued, and Anita Cantrell's voice flashed into Kathy's mind. *"There's nothing organically wrong with Larry's eyes. We don't know what triggered this awful blindness."* Jamie was impatient at Larry's silence. "Before what, Larry?"

"I don't know." His voice was vague. Now he frowned. "Don't bother me Jamie."

They finished dinner with what Neil labelled commendable speed, doing full justice to Mrs McArdle's cooking, and then piled convivially into the van for the short run to the church.

"Kathy and Larry up front," Neil ordered high spiritedly. "The girls right behind, and Jamie and Andrew in the back."

On the front seat, with Larry settled between Neil and herself, Kathy was conscious of her deepening attraction to Neil. She was drawn to him because of his strength, she chided herself. After this horrendous year behind her, she felt safe with him. A little girl clutching at a haven, she scoffed inwardly. Yet she knew — even then — that the depth of her feeling for Neil went far beyond that.

Neil swung down the driveway onto the cleared road. Moonlight lent an eerie brightness to the scalloped mountains beyond. Far to the right a beacon glowed atop a peak. Neil reached to switch on the heater, and instantly warmth oozed into the car.

"My mommie said she'd phone me tonight," Ellie remembered. All at once nervous. "Suppose she calls while we're at church?"

"Mrs McArdle will tell her — or the operator

— when you'll be back," Kathy soothed. "She'll call again."

Kathy felt the sudden surge of tension in the car. Would Anita Cantrell call Larry from Palm Beach? Would Jamie's mother call from Bermuda? Would any other parents call? When they returned to the house to trim the Christmas tree, Kathy thought, small ears would be anguishedly alert for the ring of the phone.

In minutes they were pulling up at the curb before the immaculate white Presbyterian church, dating back — a sign advised — to 1751. Parishioners were moving up the walk to the entrance. In the foyer a pair of pretty teenagers offered each arrival a candle.

Neil's party took their places in a pew near the rear of the church. Not an empty seat, Kathy noted as the services began. Later, when the congregation rose with candles in hand to sing, Kathy turned around to inspect the row of newcomers who stood behind the last pew.

Rick Jamison! He stood apart from the other late arrivals. Spontaneously Kathy smiled and lifted a hand in greeting.

Rick was alone. Nobody should be alone on Christmas Eve. Self-consciously she withdrew her gaze, turned around to collide now with Neil's quizzical gaze.

"That's someone from New York," she explained. "We met at a parkway diner coming up. He's up here for the skiing. I ran into him again at the shopping centre yesterday."

Why did she explain about meeting Rick? Why did she make an accidental encounter seem more important than it was? Suddenly she was upset.

Chapter Twelve

To avoid talking to Kathy within Larry's hearing, Randall walked out into the night before the service was over. The sounds of Christmas carols followed him from the church. He had stopped in on impulse, after dinner at a roadside restaurant — where the waiter had warned him they were closing at eight sharp.

With fleeting belligerence he had considered extending the closing time by force. But that would have been stupid. He couldn't afford to stand out around here. He was just passing through.

Why had he gone into the church? He searched his mind for an answer. Because all at once he had remembered the church out in Ohio, where he had been a choir boy. An old white building like this one, with wide lawns out front.

He remembered the Christmas, not long after his twelfth birthday, when he had hacked Donna's new English racer into pieces. She had bought it for herself from her baby-sitting money. He'd hated Donna. She never wanted him to have his way. Mom made him go to church and be a choir boy in penance.

At least he'd learned to ski out of that experience. For a little while he had enjoyed spending time with the minister. His father had been dead for two years. Nobody but women in the house.

What was Anita doing down in Palm Beach? Having herself a ball? Laughing at the way she had pushed him around? She was old. He was doing her a favour. Didn't she know that?

He slid behind the wheel of his car. He sat there for a few minutes while the motor warmed up. He should be driving that Maserati right this minute. Not this broken down pile of junk. God! Christmas Eve in a creepy town like this. What was he supposed to do with himself?

What was the name of that bar where Chris worked? Close to twenty miles from here, but nobody was on the road tonight. He'd go over and have a few beers. Think about the Christmas present he was giving to Anita. Maybe tomorrow.

He drove through town, gazing derisively at the Christmas lights strung across Main Street. A Christmas tree — a municipal effort, he assumed — was set up in an empty lot between the diner and the dry goods store. Two miles ahead, then watch for a sharp right, he remembered Chris telling him.

His head was aching again. He'd had those pills renewed just before he left. But don't mix them with booze, he warned himself. Anita wouldn't get her Christmas present.

Hell, he had to get this show on the road. Then he would feel good. Maybe Kathy would buzz him tomorrow about going up to the look-out point. Not tomorrow, he corrected himself. The next day. She wouldn't leave Larry alone tomorrow. She was one of those super-conscientious chicks.

Ten to one, when she did decide to see the view, she'd bring Larry along with her. *It would be so easy.*

He pulled up in alertness as a thick-furred white mongrel, heavy with pups, darted into the beam of the car. Trotting with a strong sense of destination. With a savage grin he stepped on the gas.

Damn! Missed the bitch.

Chapter Thirteen

The van drew up at the rear of the house. Everyone except Neil hurried out of the car and into the cozy kitchen where Mrs McArdle waited to serve them hot chocolate.

"Off with coats and settle at the table," she commanded.

The children drank with gusto, though they were eager to move into the living room to decorate the tree.

"Come on!" Jamie pushed back his chair. "Let's go fix the Christmas tree!"

Mrs McArdle had placed the box of ornaments — brought down from the attic each year — beside the freshly cut pine that brushed the high ceiling. Neil stood by with admonitions to be careful as the children took turns climbing atop chairs to reach to adorn the highest branches of the tree.

Larry sat on a hassock beside Neil and handed out the ornaments — feeling each for a moment, as though to visualise it in mind. Kathy crossed to the stereo that sat on a step table beside the sofa, moved the knob until she found a programme of Christmas carols. Her face lighted when the room reverberated with 'Joy to the World'.

The children were enjoying the evening, Kathy

decided in relief. Needing to share this realisation she swung her eyes to Neil. He was gazing at her with an earnestness that startled her.

Was Neil evaluating that moment in the church when she had exchanged greetings with Rick? Did he believe there was something between Rick and her? She didn't want Neil to think that. She wanted him to know that there was no man in her life.

Above the sound of the Christmas carols, the clatter of the children's voices, the shrillness of the phone intruded.

"I'll get it." Kathy leapt to her feet and hurried to the extension across the room.

The long-distance operator asked for Ellen. Ellie's mother, hospital-bound, had not forgotten.

"Ellie," Kathy called. All the children were motionless. Their eyes poignant. "Ellie, the call is for you."

Her face aglow Ellie darted across the room to pick up the phone.

"Mommie?"

Neil moved to the radio to lower the volume. The atmosphere in the room was tense. Neil's eyes, sombre and compassionate, travelled from one child to another.

"Why don't we all toast marshmallows?" Kathy asked blithely. She had seen the marshmallows in the kitchen earlier. "Who wants to go out to the kitchen to look for them."

"I'll go," Jamie offered as 'Joy to the World'

gave way to 'Silent Night'.

But the Christmas spirit — for five children — had been shattered.

Randall sat at the bar in the shadowed tavern. The sounds of the jukebox ricocheted about the room. Customers wandered in and out, none remaining long. He waited for Chris to return to where he sat. Another beer in tow for him.

"Can't you finish up early?" he whispered ingratiatingly. "This is a hell of a way to spend Christmas Eve."

"I'm leaving in forty minutes," Chris told him. "But I gotta go straight home. I gotta go to midnight mass with the family, or my old lady will kill me."

"What about after mass?" he pushed.

"Are you kidding?" She sighed dramatically. "I'm like under house arrest until the day after Christmas. But I'll be on the slopes the next morning." Her eyes flashed a bold invitation.

"Maybe I'll see you there," he shrugged. Noncommittal. With any luck at all he'd be on his way back to New York.

Martha would be all upset when she heard about the kid. She'd be back at the apartment right after Christmas, he recalled. He'd drop by to tell her he was leaving for California in case anyone asked for him. Maybe he'd even offer to take the car out to meet Anita at the airport. Even though he had been fired. He'd be at the cemetery to watch her bury her precious baby. And all the loot from the trust fund would go to the museum.

Randall lingered briefly. Restless. Irritated. His headache not dulled, as he had hoped, by the round of beers. What the hell was he doing hanging around Chris? What could she do for him?

Since he was sixteen, he had realised women existed to make life more exciting for him. Like the widow whose lawns he mowed that summer and whose driveway he shovelled in the winter, until she married that lawyer and moved to Florida. When he wasn't mowing or shovelling, he was under the sheets with her. Mom got all uptight because the widow let him borrow her car so much. Mom complained he was charging the old girl too much money. Mom didn't know the services he was rendering.

Randall drove back to the motel. Every room was dark. Only one parking space occupied tonight. A truck with multi-state plates, on a long haul. His face tightened. Like the truck that sent him to that stinking hospital.

The motel unit was heated electrically. He pushed the heat to 'High' with a grin. Let them pay a fancy electric bill. They charged enough for these lousy units. He stripped to jockey shorts, pulled down the covers, and flipped on the TV.

Hell, only three channels up here. Nothing on that he'd cared to watch. But he left the set on as he rummaged through his flight bag for the novel he had lifted from Anita's room. Another Stephen King.

The book in hand he settled himself on the bed and flipped to the first page. Anita said it was great. What he really liked were those gory historicals about the Christians being thrown to the lions before those Roman big wheels.

In the small but pleasantly furnished living room of his brownstone apartment in the West '80s, David Ames flipped off the TV and lowered his lean, muscular length into a corner of the sofa. He'd never give up his Manhattan apartment, he promised himself. This was home. He'd only begun charging around the world on assignments after he lost his custody battle to Anita.

Up till now he'd always contrived to be in town for the periods when he had custody of Larry. It was rotten to be separated from his kid on Christmas Eve. He glanced at the clock on the fireplace mantle. Christmas Day, he corrected himself. OK, he was chucking that whole scene. It wasn't helping him to race all over in the months he didn't have custody. Whatever it cost, he was going back into court and demand weekend visits along with what had been awarded him.

Damn, where the hell was Larry? Anita's apartment was closed up. Nobody answered at the East Hampton house nor at his ex-mother-in-law's apartment. He'd rushed back the moment he'd finished up — working twenty hours a day this past week. *Somebody* must be around in the city to tell him where Anita had taken Larry for the holidays. Who, he asked himself in towering frustration.

Chapter Fourteen

Kathy came awake slowly. She was conscious of the cozy warmth in the room, the comfort of the mound of blankets that embraced her. Then the pleasurable moments were destroyed by the sound of a raucous crash close by. Instantly she was fully awake.

She pulled herself up on one elbow, squinted in concentration. Snow following from the roof, she told herself in relief. Probably pulling a loose segment of slate to the ground. Last night Neil had warned her that sometimes happened. How childish of her to have been unnerved by it.

She left the studio couch, went into the bedroom to look in on Larry. He was sound asleep. The falling snow had not disturbed him. She felt a surge of tenderness as she pulled up the blankets he'd tossed aside.

She crossed to the window. No sunlight filtered through the sides of the shades this morning. Had there been fresh snow last night?

She pulled the shade aside for a view of the outdoors. Fresh snow on the driveway obliterated the car tracks. Animal prints were etched deep in the whiteness. Another couple of inches must have fallen overnight. The sky appeared indecisive about unleashing yet another load.

Christmas morning. Almost 9 A.M. She listened intently. No sounds in the house. The children were all asleep, she realised with astonishment.

When Robin and she were little, they were up at six on Christmas morning. All at once she was flooded by nostalgia. Mom said they had celebrated one Christmas morning at a few minutes past 3 A.M. Robin had been awakened and rebelliously insisted on opening Christmas presents.

Kathy gathered together a cluster of clothes and toilet articles and went to the bathroom to wash and dress. By the time she arrived in the kitchen, Mrs McArdle was cutting biscuits and Neil was removing ashes from the Franklin stove.

"Merry Christmas," she said exuberantly. Neil and Mrs McArdle swung around with bright smiles.

"Merry Christmas, Kathy," Mrs McArdle echoed and moved to the range where deep amber liquid bubbled in the percolator top. "Sit down and have some coffee."

"Merry Christmas, Kathy." Neil's eyes made this a special moment.

"I gather there was more snow last night." Kathy was both exhilarated and unnerved by the glow in Neil's eyes. *This was happening too fast.*

"I'll take the children up to the pond after we've gone through the package-opening scene," Neil decided. Like her he was concerned that the children were not barging into the living room in the normal pursuit of presents. The present each wanted most was not available. "We'll shovel and skate," he said with an effort at humour, "until we have a good clear path all around the pond."

"I forgot to phone my sister last night," Kathy remembered in dismay. "Is it all right if I call from here? I'll ask the operator for the charges."

Neil chuckled. "The school can absorb the cost of the call. Go ahead."

Kathy glanced at her watch. "I'd better wait a while. They're out in Texas. It's — what? — three hours earlier out there?"

Neil nodded. "I called my folks last night out in California." His eyes were warm. "My two brothers and their wives and a collection of three kids arrived yesterday. Everybody belabouring the lack of snow. They're about forty miles above San Diego."

"I was nervous about driving up here in the snow." For a moment Kathy hovered on the brink of telling Neil about their accident on the Taconic. But no. Why talk about a freakish accident like that on Christmas day? "But I'm glad we came."

While they ate satin-scrambled eggs and burnished sausages, the children began to trickle into the kitchen. Again Kathy was conscious that they showed no desire to rush into the living room, where presents lay stacked in a calculated disarray beneath the tree.

"Where's Larry?" Ellie asked with proprietary interest. Little Ellie, Kathy thought with tenderness, who would be a perfect mother some day. "Is he still asleep?"

"I think so," Kathy said. Should she go in to check on Larry?

"Let me wake him," Ellie coaxed. "We have to eat breakfast before we get our presents. Don't we, Neil?" she demanded with more enthusiasm than that displayed by the others. Because, Kathy realised, last night Ellie's mother had bothered to telephone her.

"Sure. Go in and wake Larry," Neil encouraged. Kathy's eyes darted uncertainly to him. He nodded with quiet reassurance. "And lay out his clothes for him. Tell him you'll be back in a few minutes to show him the way downstairs."

Kathy was uneasy, though, until the two children returned to the kitchen. Ellie calmly leading Larry by the hand. For the first time since going blind, Larry had dressed himself.

"Last Christmas," Larry said with poignant wistfulness as he sat at the table, "I was with my daddy at St Thomas. We had a little house right by the ocean. And we brought an itsy-bitsy Christmas tree with us on the plane."

They ate, then moved into the living room. Now the children were eager for Christmas booty, Kathy discovered with relief. A facsimile, she thought sentimentally, of what was happening in houses all over Salem.

With much levity gifts were distributed. The Christmas atmosphere was almost real.

"That's your present from Mrs Holmes,"

91

Kathy explained while Larry pulled aside the wrappings. Larry's presents from his mother and father had been opened earlier and remained at the apartment.

Larry felt inside the box with absorbing curiosity.

"It's a toy car!" he said. "Mommie gave me one, and Daddy, too. And a record player and lots of records and new ice-skates," he recalled. "What's your present?"

"Here it is, darling." Kathy put the box into Larry's hands. "Open it. Tell me what it is."

She waited, listening to the warm response of the other children to their own gifts. All of them surprised and touchingly pleased that she had remembered them. She watched while Larry opened her gift and felt the contents.

"It's a toy animal!" Larry's voice deepened with delight. "He's so little! What kind is he?" He moved his fingers along the drooping ears, down to the short legs. "Kathy, what is he?"

"He's a dachshund puppy. You know how they look," she encouraged. "What are you going to call him?"

"Malcolm," Larry said decisively after a moment. "Daddy used to tell me about a dog he had when he was little. His name was Malcolm." He hesitated. "Kathy, do they have phones in Rio?"

"Yes." Kathy's throat tightened with anger at Larry's father. "But sometimes on holidays like Christmas it's impossible to get a call through because so many people are trying to make calls."

"Do you think Daddy tried to call me?"

"I'm sure he did," Kathy said. Conscious that Andrew and Jean were sombrely tuned in to her conversation with Larry. "Lots of parents must have been so disappointed that they couldn't get through."

Neil organised the children in a word game that had been his present to Jamie. Kathy took advantage of this activity to go into the kitchen to phone Robin. With a baby in the house they must be up despite the time difference.

"I told Agnes there was no need for her to come out on Christmas morning," Mrs McArdle said as Kathy reached for the phone. "The kids make up their own beds, and I can do what straightening has to be done. But I'll go check on the bedrooms, just in case." Mrs McArdle was providing her with privacy for her phone call, Kathy thought gratefully.

Her heart pounded in anticipation as she heard the phone ring in Robin's suburban Texas house. She had not seen Robin since August. It seemed a shockingly long time.

"Hello." Robin's voice held the remembered touch of effervescence.

"Merry Christmas, Robbie." She had not called her sister Robbie since she was eleven.

"Kathy, baby!" Pleasure laced Robin's voice. "Your presents arrived day before yesterday. Everything's gorgeous! I was so angry with myself for not having taken down your phone number up in the country so I could call. I just know you're in Salem, New York, at some school. It seems weird not being with you at Christmas."

"I miss you all. But we're so busy with the children there's not much time to be lonely."

"We've been listening to the TV news, hearing about all the snow back East. Did you have any trouble driving up? I was worrying about that."

"It was snowing, but the roads were cleared." Where was that crazy drunk now? Cold sober and having a great Christmas dinner with his wife and family? Did he even remember that he almost killed two people on the highway? But that was over. Why couldn't she blot it out of her mind? "The trip just took longer than I had expected."

"Kathy . . ." Robin was hesitant. "You're not moping over the break-up with Clint?" Robin had never met Clint, but she'd heard much about him.

"Robin, no." Conviction in her voice. "I'm glad it's over. It was wrong for me." But at first she had been terribly shaken. And then she had met Neil.

"Anybody interesting up there?" Robin seemed to read her mind.

"Sort of," she hedged and Robin laughed.

"Well, you don't waste time." But Robin was pleased.

"Nothing serious," Kathy insisted. "I just meant I won't be bored these nine days up here."

But she wished with a startling intensity that these nine days could be stretched out endlessly.

"Write me when you get back to the city. Tell me everything that's been happening," Robin ordered.

"I will," Kathy promised. "Now tell me about the baby. When do I receive new snapshots?"

With an eye to the cost of the call Kathy got off the phone in a few minutes. But her face glowed when she returned to the living room. It had been wonderful to hear Robin's voice on Christmas morning.

"I'm taking everybody up to the pond to skate," Neil greeted her. "No sun out yet, but they'll warm up from the exercise fast enough. All right," he turned to the others, "go get your jackets, gloves, and skates."

"I'll get yours, Larry," Kathy said. Watching Larry's face.

"No," he rejected. "I don't want to go."

Kathy's eyes sought Neil's. He gestured her not to coax Larry.

"All right. Let's listen to some music," Kathy said with casual acceptance.

Perhaps later Larry and she would go up to the pond alone. Larry was nervous about skating with others when he couldn't see. But with the two of them alone on the pond, he might feel less self-conscious.

The house vibrated with a surge of high spirits as the children scurried about collecting the necessary skating paraphernalia. Larry settled himself in a Boston rocker and cradled tiny Malcolm in his arms.

"Larry, won't you come with us?" Ellie coaxed. "I'll hold your hand."

"I don't want to skate," Larry insisted. "I'd rather stay here and play with Malcolm."

"OK," Ellie accepted.

With the children gone, the house seemed suddenly desolate. Larry sat motionless in his rocker — clutching Malcolm in a poignant silence. Kathy fought against a wave of frustration. She must not allow Larry to spend the whole vacation sitting indoors! But yesterday, she reminded herself, Neil had persuaded Larry to go on the wagon ride with the others. He would arrange other outings, and Larry would participate in them. Neil was so good with the kids.

Why did she allow Neil to monopolise her thoughts this way? She didn't want to be hurt again. And with Neil it could be a thousand times more painful than it had been with Clint.

"Larry, I'm dying to go up and see the view from the mountains just outside of town," she fabricated enthusiastically. She must do something to get Larry out of the house. Where was that place? Rick Jamison had mentioned it. "Would you mind if we drove up there now?" Her voice was ingratiatingly appealing.

"OK." Larry's air of resignation tugged at Kathy.

"I met someone at the shopping centre who knows the perfect spot," Kathy continued. Going with Rick would make it a special occasion, she told herself. "I'll phone him and ask him to take us up there." Of course, Rick might not be at the motel, Kathy conceded. But having Rick with them would make it seem like a party. "You stay here with Malcolm. I'll go upstairs to look for the phone number."

She hurried upstairs — visualising the view that awaited them. Bromley, Manchester, and Bennington, Rick said. It must be sensational.

In their suite she pulled her handbag from a dresser drawer and rummaged for the folded-over napkin with Rick's phone number. Where was it? Oh, here it was! With the napkin in one hand she headed back for the living room. Larry sat in the rocker without moving. Fondling one of Malcolm's ears with his small fingers.

Kathy dialled, waited expectantly for someone to answer. It was funny how she had bumped into Rick at the shopping centre. Both of them on the Taconic night before last, stopping off at that diner. Then his popping up that way at the church. She'd remembered him because of his jacket that was exactly like Clint's.

"Hello." A bored male voice greeted her.

"Rick Jamison, please."

"Hold on. I'll buzz him."

Rick might be on the slopes. He'd said he was expecting a buddy from New York. He might not be in the mood to go to the look-out point. She hoped he was at the motel and available. All at once she was eager to be out of the house in the cold brisk air.

"Sorry," the man at the switchboard reported. "He don't answer. Maybe he went skiing."

"Thank you." Kathy put down the phone and walked back to the fireplace to sit beside Larry. She was disappointed that Rick wasn't available. "I suppose we don't go to the look-out point today," she laughed. "He wasn't home when I called." She leaned forward and reached for one of Larry's hands. "Why don't we wait until the others come back from the pond, and go up there by ourselves? Just the two of us. Nobody on the ice but you and me," she emphasised. "We'll skate all by ourselves."

"I might fall," Larry said after a moment.

"I might fall, too," Kathy pointed out. "What does it matter?" She managed a chuckle. "We'll pick ourselves up and go on skating." Anita Cantrell said Larry skated well. He had taken lessons regularly last winter. While he still had his sight. "We'll go up for just a little while," she coaxed. "Until Mrs McArdle is ready to serve lunch. OK?"

Larry frowned indecisively for a moment.

"OK," he capitulated.

Chapter Fifteen

Randall checked the mileometer for the distance he had travelled from the motel. The manager said there would be a diner open eight miles out this way. It was rough to find a place to eat up here on Christmas Day.

Should he have hung around the motel to see if Kathy would call him? No. She said she'd be all tied up with the kid today. After breakfast he would drive over to the school. Roam about the property. Take the rifle along just in case.

Maybe Kathy would persuade Larry to go out on the ice. Without the others. Larry wouldn't go on the pond with anybody but Kathy around. Anita said she couldn't get him to go skating this winter at Rockefeller Plaza because of the people around.

He hunched over the wheel, stared hard to the left. A white, blue-trimmed diner sat fifty feet back from the road. That was it. He swung off the road into the parking area. There were only three cars out front. And those probably belonged to the help, he guessed with a spurt of humour. But what difference would it make to him, as long as they served him a decent breakfast? Best meal of the day.

The windows of the diner, decorated with Christmas wreaths, were steamed over. He opened the door and walked into the inviting inner warmth. The counter was deserted except for a heavy-set man in a red flannel jacket and red hunting cap. He was flirting with an elderly but youthfully-coiffed waitress. The booths were empty.

Randall settled himself in a corner booth and reached for the menu. The waitress came over to the table with a broad smile.

"Merry Christmas and *bon appetite*." She welcomed him with a look of overt admiration. Thirty years ago, Randall thought, she must have been gorgeous. The legs were still great.

"Orange juice, pancakes, sausages, and keep the coffee coming," Randall drawled while she poured for him.

"I like a man who knows how to eat," she quipped.

He leaned back and sipped the strong, fresh coffee. He was restless. Time was moving too fast. He wanted to have this deal over with, to be able to cut back to New York. Maybe he'd be lucky today.

All he needed was two minutes alone with Larry and Kathy. Maybe they would take a walk through the woods. Or go sledging on that sharp incline behind the pond. Just the two of them. Maybe they'd go skating alone. *It would be so easy*.

He wasted no time over breakfast. Eating with relish. Finding satisfaction in his feeling of direction. Go to the school area. Park by the side of the road like he meant to do some hunting in the woods. He smiled faintly. He *was* going hunting. For big game.

After he'd eaten, he left the diner and drove to Salem. He turned left at the traffic light and followed the deserted road out of the village limits. He would pull off the road a couple hundred feet before the beginning of the school property.

He passed a parked van and saw a cluster of red-capped hunters disappearing into the woods far to the left. A pack of dogs barked raucously.

Make sure the geese were out front, he reminded himself. If they weren't, he'd never be able to get close to the house. This time of day they ought to be out of the pen. He slowed down, cut off at the left a few hundred feet beyond the van. The school property clearly began just ahead.

He emerged from the car, walked around to the boot, unlocked it. He reached beneath the blanket for the 7 mm 'custom' model Remington that had set him back a chunk of loot. So it was a big gun to use in small-game season. No law said he couldn't use it for hunting possums.

The gun under his arm, Randall walked along the edge of the road. His camping boots left deep tracks in the snow. The character at the motel said there was an outdoor range not far from here. He smiled in pride. He didn't need practice. He was a crack shot. With the sight on the Remington he could hit accurately at two hundred feet. Given the opportunity he would kill the kid with the first bullet.

The air was cold. Damp. The sky promised more snow. Occasional attempts of the sun to break through were halfhearted. Weak. He walked briskly. No headache nagging at him today. He was stimulated by the prospect of a possible encounter with his quarry. He wouldn't miss.

Two hundred feet ahead the pair of geese pattered across the sprawling front lawn. They were pecking at the bark on the trunk of an enormous old tree now. Randall cut out purposefully across the road, then disappeared into the woods that belonged to the school. He'd have no trouble with the geese. Just let Kathy come out with the kid. The two of them alone.

He sauntered into the woods, walking parallel with the road in the general direction of the pond. A cat darted across his line of vision. He lifted the rifle, making a pretense of aiming at the cat.

He hated cats. He smiled in sardonic amusement as he remembered a mangy tabby cat that used to hang around the house the summer he was twelve. His sisters always fed it, but Mom wouldn't allow a cat in the house. He got bronchitis from cat fur.

He remembered the day the rest of the family went to a church picnic. He stayed at home. He hated going places with the family. The cat came meowing around. He put out a saucer of tuna. Not being philanthropic. As soon as the cat moved close to the saucer — before it could reach for the tuna, he dropped a sack over its head.

Wow, that crazy cat carried on when he tied a piece of rope about the top of the sack! It went nuts trying to push its way out. At first he wasn't sure what he was going to do with that damn cat. It would give him no thrill to drown it. People did that all the time. Then all at once he had known what he was going to do.

He took the cat, in the sack, behind the garage. And while it tried to fight its way out of the sack, he dug a deep hole in the ground. He buried that cat alive. Later he planted a coleus there. Mom said it was the prettiest coleus she ever saw . . .

Randall paused. Stiffened into alertness. He could see the house below. He could hear the sounds of the kids indoors. Somebody was walking away from the house — towards the pond. Two figures. Larry and Kathy.

With a sense of triumph he moved noiselessly, watching to avoid the winter-brittle boughs that lay across the ground. This wasn't a time to advertise his presence. At a hundred fifty feet he stopped, positioned himself behind a sagging corner of the barn. From here he had an unobstructed view of the pond.

Kathy was helping the kid on with his skates. Randall watched while she tied the laces into place, then leaned against a tree trunk to change from her walking boots to skates.

Kathy and Larry stepped out onto the ice hand in hand. He lifted the gun to his shoulder. Look through the sight. There Larry was, centred on the crosshair. Randall held his breath, poised his finger to press the trigger. He felt hot and cold with excitement.

OK, Anita. Here comes your Christmas present!

Chapter Sixteen

"Larry, there's a squirrel starting up the tree," Kathy said in a semi-whisper, lest the squirrel be frightened. "Oh!"

In her excitement Kathy slipped. She fell to the ice, pulled Larry down with her. Simultaneously she heard the report of a gun. Sprawled on the ice — still clutching Larry's hand in hers — she saw the sudden splotch of red flowing through the squirrel's fur as it tumbled to the ground.

"Kathy," Larry reproached, "you pulled me down. I wouldn't have fallen."

"I know, darling," Kathy soothed. "I'm sorry. I should have let go of your hand." Her mind was racing to an unnerving realisation. *Someone behind them had shot that squirrel.* "Larry, did you hurt yourself?" she asked solicitously.

"I'm all right," Larry said. "But I wouldn't have fallen if you hadn't pulled me down."

Shaken less from the fall than from realising a hunter was in shooting distance, Kathy pulled herself erect again and helped Larry to his feet. The shot had come from the woods there. How could any hunter take such a chance with human lives? He must have seen them on the pond!

He was afraid to come forward to claim his quarry. He knew he was hunting on private property, posted against hunting. He could be fined for this. Involuntarily she shivered. He might have hit Larry or her. He'd be guilty of manslaughter.

"Kathy?" Neil's voice rang through the stillness. "Are Larry and you all right?" He was running towards the pond.

"We're all right," Kathy reported with an effort at humour. "But the squirrel's not doing too well."

"What happened to the squirrel?" Larry asked anxiously. "Did somebody shoot him?" Belatedly he was aware of the gunshot.

"He was frightened and ran away," Kathy improvised. "The hunter missed him."

"I heard the shot." Neil was furious. "Can't they read? We've got signs posted all around the acreage!"

"He frightened away the squirrel on the tree there." She mimed to Neil that Larry was unaware the small animal had been killed. "Just at the moment that I fell and pulled Larry down with me." Now she was trembling. How close they had come to being shot!

"Nobody's ever tried this before. They know the children roam the grounds." He paused, his eyes moving about the pond. "Where were you when the shot was fired?"

"Right here."

"Where do you think the shot came from?"

"From the woods behind us."

Neil's eyes met hers, telegraphing his realisation that they had been in the line of fire. If she had not slipped on the ice — if she had not pulled

106

Larry down with her, one of them might have stopped the bullet rather than the squirrel. Neil's face tightened in quiet rage.

"I'm going down to talk to the police. We won't tolerate this kind of trespassing. For the rest of the day we'd better keep the children close to the house. Until we find out what kind of idiots are roaming around here with guns."

"We'll skate tomorrow, Larry," Kathy promised. "Mrs McArdle must be about ready to serve lunch now, anyway."

While Larry asked questions about the squirrel, whose body Neil was cautiously removing from the vicinity of the pond, Kathy took off Larry's ice-skates, helped him on with his boots, then performed the same chore for herself. The squirrel could not be buried in the frozen ground, but other animals would dispose of the remains fast enough.

"No, I don't think a squirrel would make a good pet," Kathy replied to Larry's enquiry. "And I don't think we could have caught him, anyway."

"Kathy, would you like to go down with me to talk to the police?" Neil asked as they walked back to the house. "You'll be able to tell them exactly what happened."

"All right." She still felt shaken. Again, they had been so close to death. What a crazy happening, right on top of that idiotic drunk on the Taconic. "But I didn't see anyone. It all happened too fast."

Now she re-ran in her mind — in slow motion — the minute details of what had happened. She fell. She pulled Larry down on the ice with her — simultaneously with the shot. They lay there on the ground, and she saw the blood oozing from the squirrel. She shivered. It could have been Larry or her.

Despite the cold Mrs McArdle stood at the open kitchen door. Her face showed her anxiety.

"What was a hunter doing so close to the house?" she demanded indignantly.

"After small game," Neil reported. "But he didn't have the nerve to take possession of this one."

"Is this small-game season?" Kathy asked curiously.

"That's right." Neil nodded. "Deer and bear are out of season. Of course," he added wryly, "squirrels are an unprotected species. They can be shot at any time."

"You'll talk to the game warden?" Mrs McArdle asked. "You know it's city folks making this kind of trouble. Local folks know better."

"After lunch," Neil promised, "Kathy and I are driving over to the State Police. You won't mind keeping an eye on the children for a little while?"

"You know I won't," she clucked, and Kathy saw a glint in her eyes that said Mrs McArdle was not above suspecting a romantic angle to their trip to the State Police.

Without mentioning that the squirrel had been killed, Neil told the children that they were to remain close to the house for the rest of the day until he was sure the word was around that nobody was to poach on the school property.

"Say, what about some snowmobiling around the fields across the road this afternoon?" he proposed with a show of high spirits. "We have permission to snowmobile there. I'll stop in town and see about borrowing the one we had before."

The response was noisily enthusiastic.

"All right, everybody," Mrs McArdle ordered briskly. "Go wash up for lunch."

None of the children was alarmed about what had happened on the pond, Kathy thought gratefully as she helped Larry cut up his food. How close she had come to these children in such a short span of time! How close she felt to Neil . . .

Chapter Seventeen

Randall drove through town without direction. His knuckles were white from the tightness with which he gripped the wheel. He was furious with himself for another failure. But he had to hold on to his temper. That was his big problem. Always had been. *Cool it man.*

If she hadn't fallen on the ice and pulled the kid down with her, Larry would be dead. He had Larry on the sight for that one second. He couldn't have missed if she hadn't fallen! Damn! He'd been a hairline from accomplishing his mission.

He lightened his foot on the accelerator. No sense in getting picked up for speeding here. And his tracks in the snow, back there at the school, were being covered by the fresh snow that was falling now. He was in the clear.

Watch the temper. Don't let that cause trouble. Always his problem, he reiterated in irritation. That was why he dropped out of school. That bastard of a professor at UCLA — so arrogant when he said his grade ought to be changed. He hated being a B student. It had to be straight A's. He had to be the best.

He'd worked his butt off in the course, and all he got on that paper was a B. His mouth tightened as he remembered how he'd ripped the report into shreds and thrown it on the floor at the professor's feet. And then he picked up a metal bookend and tossed it through a closed window.

"That was a hostile act," the professor remarked with that infuriating calm of his. "I'll let you get away with it this time because I think you need help. You go to the campus psychiatrist, and I'll cover for you."

"Why do I have to go to a psychiatrist?" he demanded belligerently. He had only contempt for shrinks.

"Because if you don't," the professor said quietly, "you're going to have a devil of time explaining why you deliberately destroyed school property."

He went to the shrink because he was frightened of his temper. Remembering that session, he winced.

"What's troubling you?" the psychiatrist had asked.

"I don't know," he said uneasily. "My temper bothers me — the way I hit out sometimes. It's rough in school. All the competition for grades. All the pressures. I'm always fighting to hold on to my temper." He said nothing about the headaches. He was ashamed of the headaches. It indicated a physical weakness.

The shrink let him talk. After the first few minutes he invented. Why should he spill his guts to this creep? The shrink made an appointment for him the following week, but he never returned. In three weeks he had dropped out of UCLA.

Nobody knew he meant to kill Larry. They'd blame it on some crazy hunter. Those accidents happened every year. But he'd have to stay away from the property for the next day or two — till this cooled off.

All right, stay away from the property. Figure out how to do it some place else. Find a way to see Kathy again. Work out an angle where he could pick off the kid away from the school property.

You can do it. Put the old brain to work.

Chapter Eighteen

Snow was coming down steadily as Kathy and Neil walked out of the house and to the van. She slid onto the front seat while Neil circled around to climb behind the wheel. All through lunch, truant, disturbing thoughts had invaded her mind. Had that bullet been meant for her? First that business on the Taconic, now this. Less than forty-eight hours later.

No! Don't be melodramatic. It was one of those weird coincidences. This was hunting country. Hunting and sports were the big deals up here. It was a different way of life. Kathy shuddered. She loathed guns.

"The State Police don't take kindly to this sort of invasion," Neil assured her. "I doubt that they'll be able to pick anybody up, but they'll circulate word among the hunters that they'll be in serious trouble poaching on school property."

"They know about the children. The school sign hangs right there at the side of the road." Kathy sighed in frustration. "How do they dare take chances like that? Just to hit a squirrel." Had the squirrel been their intended victim? No, stop this melodrama. Nobody was out to kill her.

"You always find a lunatic fringe." Neil smiled wryly. "I remember when my sister and her husband had a house with five acres up in northern

New Jersey, before they moved out to California. They had a magnificent chunk of property. The house sat on a slight hill with an acre of lawn rolling down to woods and a pond. Below there was a wooded ravine and a big plateau."

"Sounds beautiful," Kathy said.

"I loved the place. But it was prime hunting country. Deer used to come down to the pond for the food Fred put out for them. I was there one weekend in hunting season, sprawled on the deck reading the *Sunday Times* while the two kids played on the lawn. Would you believe, two hunters came right out of the woods onto the lawn with their guns aimed at a woodchuck." He grinned reminiscently. "I told them to get out quick before I put a bullet through their heads. Fred right away called the State Troopers. Most people respect the 'No Hunting' signs, but there's the handful of nuts who don't." His eyes left the wheel; for an instant. "I don't mind admitting I was scared when I heard that shot so close to the house. I knew Larry and you were on the ice." His eyes shone with disconcerting ardour.

"I'm surprised you don't have dogs about the place." Kathy's heart was pounding. She was up here for a few days more, she rebuked herself. That was all. No time to become romantically involved with Neil.

"Mrs Prentiss, who owns the school, was so upset when the last dog was killed chasing cars that she swore she'd have no more. That's why she got geese," he chuckled. "They're great as

114

watch dogs except when they're loose and on the front lawn." He hesitated. "I'll have a week's winter vacation late in February. I thought of going down to New York. Could we have dinner and go to the theatre or the opera? I'm an opera nut. Would you like to go to the Met while I'm down there?"

"I've never been to the opera." Kathy's face was incandescent. "I'd love to go with you."

"I'm not trampling on anybody's toes?" he asked after a moment.

"I've no commitments." She was casual on the surface. Hiding the exhilaration that surged through her. Clint belonged to yesterday.

"Great." Neil smiled. He moved one hand from the wheel to rest over hers for an instant.

Kathy leaned back against the seat. Caught up in conflicting emotions. Elation. Unease. Anticipation. She had come to Salem running from a broken relationship. She must not run headlong into another without being convinced it was real.

Now Neil was talking about his last summer vacation in Spain. She listened with an air of avid interest, but part of her mind grappled with her emotions.

"Valencia was astonishing. The water was like a warm bath. When you came out, salt was all over you. And that current!" He whistled eloquently. "You'd go out at one stretch of beach and come back in two hundred yards down."

Neil pulled off the road before the State Police headquarters. Kathy and he went in to talk about the trespassing at the school.

"If you could have got us over there while they were on the property, we could have done something." The policeman was apologetic. "You didn't even get a look at him?" he asked Kathy.

"I was sprawled on my face on the ice," Kathy reminded. "No. I didn't see him."

"We'll talk to the game warden, spread the word around that we're on the watch for trespassers. You see anything, call us fast."

Again, in the car, Kathy dallied with the thought of expressing the suspicions that kept pushing into her mind. But, no. It was ridiculous to think there might be some connection between what happened on the Taconic and the incident with the squirrel.

Nobody tried to kill her. Who would want to kill her?

Chapter Nineteen

Randall walked naked out of the shower and stood before the mirror that hung above the dresser. Satisfied with his reflections. Since he was fourteen, he had enjoyed the sight of his naked body. He wore his clothes so tight they were like another skin. Mom used to raise hell about that.

Why did Chris have to be scared to go out tonight? It was a hell of a way to spend Christmas night. Alone in a motel. He'd go out for dinner. Afterwards he'd look for some old Charles Bronson movie. So he might have to drive forty or fifty miles each way. Maybe near Saratoga Springs or up to Glens Falls. What did he have to lose? There was nothing else he could do tonight.

He'd find some place open for dinner, pick up a local newspaper and search for a movie. He'd relax tonight. Tomorrow he would be back at his rounds.

Maybe he ought to stop playing fancy games. Just sneak up on the house. Throw a stick of dynamite into the kitchen. In the country you buy dynamite and no questions asked. All you had to do was pretend you wanted to blow up a tree. All at once he was tingling with excitement.

No, he warned himself. If I buy dynamite, somebody might remember me. Don't take chances. That was the smart way to play this game.

I could make a home-made bomb. I've got the bullets. All I'd have to do would be to empty the gunpowder into a container. Stick in a fuse. Seal it off. Throw it into a room where Larry is.

Wow, that would make the headlines! On the TV news and everything! No. That's not what I want. Just the kid. And if necessary, the girl.

I want the spotlight on little Larry Ames. Poor little rich boy, whose mommie won't be so rich once he's dead.

Randall rolled over on his back, stretched, yawned as the alarm on his travel clock signalled that it was 6 A.M. He opened his eyes. It was still dark out. The sun wouldn't rise for a while this time of year.

He considered his plans for the day. He would spend some time on the slopes before he got down to business. Nobody out there this time of morning, he remembered with relish. Anywhere was God's country when you were on the side of a mountain alone.

He threw aside the blankets. Rose to his feet and switched on the lamp that sat on the night table. In the low-wattage glow he turned to inspect the calendar. Each night — for three nights — he had crossed off a date with his pen. Maybe tonight he could pack up and head back to New York. If he was smart.

He washed and dressed with a speed motivated

by a desire for coffee. Two or three cups of coffee and he'd be clear-eyed enough for the slopes. Last night he had stopped to chat for a while with the motel manager. The manager said if he drove into Cambridge, he could get hot rolls and coffee any time after six in the morning.

He opened the door of his unit and walked out into the raw, early morning cold. A night sky was still on display, wearing a hint of fresh snow. He walked to the car, slid behind the wheel. The motor was cold. It would take a few minutes to warm up.

He turned the ignition key, pumped the accelerator. Impatiently he waited for the motor to respond. The car was dank and uncomfortable without the heater in action. An air of desolation enveloped the outdoors. The other units of the motel were blacked out. Only three other cars were in residence.

He grunted in annoyance that the car was taking so long to warm up. This would never happen if he had the Maserati. Damn Anita! But she was going to be sorry. Too bad she couldn't know who killed the kid. She was getting her Christmas present from him late — but she would get it.

The motor was humming now. He rolled out of the parking area onto the road. Not a car was moving. It was early even for skiers. He watched now for signs that would lead him into Cambridge. He'd have coffee, go on the slopes for a while. That would shove his mind into high gear.

His best bet was to inveigle Kathy away from

the house — with Larry. Why the devil hadn't she called yesterday about going out to the lookout point? She'd seemed interested. Like he'd guessed, she was too conscientious about the job.

He turned into Cambridge. In his mind he went over the directions for reaching King's. The streets were still night dark. Here and there a figure hunched against the cold, en route to work. Most of the houses showed no indication of life.

Anybody could move into this town and massacre it at this hour of the morning, and nobody would know. The whole place could be set on fire before they struggled into wakefulness, and he could stand on a corner here and gun them down as they staggered out of their burning house. *One man could do that.*

Randall leaned forward to inspect the left side of the street. That was King's Bakery right there. The small, neat white building, surprisingly cheerful in appearance. He parked on the right, left the car, crossed the street and walked up the narrow path that led to the entrance.

He opened the door and walked into the tempting aromas of freshly baked bread, of cakes in the oven. The bakery counters were set up in a right angle on the right. Attractive wooden tables and chairs on the left. To the rear, on a slightly elevated level, was the counter. The walls were colourfully papered in a colonial pattern that lent an air of vitality to the store.

A quartet of patrons — obviously hunters — sat at a table for four. The place was otherwise empty except for a pair of girls behind the counter. He sat at a table for two, turning on the Randall Brooks charm for the girl who came to take his order.

"You serve breakfast?" he asked leisurely. He knew they didn't. Cake or rolls with coffee, tea, or milk.

"I'm sorry," the girl apologized. "We have the cakes there . . ."

She pointed to a tray. "And doughnuts and Vienna rolls and —"

"Give me about four Vienna rolls and coffee," he said briskly. "And keep the coffee coming."

He would stay on the slopes for a couple of hours, leave before Chris arrived. Tomorrow, let Chris find him there. She'd be back looking for him, he guessed complacently. Today he would station himself in the car down the road from the school — when he left the slopes — and keep a watch for Kathy.

She had to leave the house sometime. He would follow her, connive a date. Invite her for lunch somewhere. Maybe over in Manchester. That might be stronger bait than the look-out point, he decided with rising optimism.

He would follow the original plan. Arrange to have her pick him up in her car, with the kid. Only on the way they would have a terrible accident. Didn't they know the woods up here were full of hunters?

Nobody suspected anything yesterday. This, too, would be just another coincidence. Even if

121

the cops got any ideas, they couldn't prove anything. He'd be back at his motel. Waiting for Kathy to pick him up. A hundred to one she wouldn't tell anybody at the house exactly who was taking her to lunch. Besides, she didn't know his real name. Nobody up here knew. He'd be home free.

Chapter Twenty

Kathy lay in bed long after she awoke. Last night she had encountered difficulty in falling asleep. When sleep finally overtook her, it was slumber fraught with disturbing dreams.

She was falling in love with Neil. She wasn't ready to fall in love again. How could she know it was real? She had thought she was in love with Clint, but it had been only a need to be close to someone. She had been shaken by her parents' death. Frightened by her aloneness in the world.

She was haunted irregularly by the conviction that there could be something fine for Neil and her. She was drawn to his warmth, his dedication to his work, his tenderness. There had been no tenderness in Clint.

Clint had kept her on the edge of her seat. She was never entirely at ease with him. With Neil she felt safe, cherished. He wanted to see her down in New York. He saw a future for them.

Before Larry and she left Salem, she must make up her mind about seeing more of Neil. Could she find a permanent relationship with Neil? No mistakes. She couldn't bear the prospect of being hurt again.

She left her bed, reached for her robe, and walked to the door of the bedroom. Larry stirred and without opening his eyes reached for Malcolm. Tears welled in Kathy. Would Larry ever see again?

"Kathy?" That urgency in Larry's voice that accompanied each awakening to a dark world.

"I'm here, Larry. Shall we get up now and go downstairs for breakfast?"

"Yes," Larry said with a new assurance. "Ellie and I are going to play her records this morning."

Kathy and Larry dressed and went downstairs to the kitchen. Larry clutched Malcolm snugly in his arms. The stuffed dachshund was his constant companion. Ellie and Jamie were at the breakfast table with Neil.

"I thought you'd sleep all morning," Neil teased Kathy and Larry. "And we were going to eat all the cornbread ourselves. Real cornbread made with sweet cream."

"I adore it," Kathy said gaily. She plucked a piece from the plate and put it into Larry's hand and took another for herself. Why did she have this feeling that the whole world had brightened because she was sitting at the breakfast table beside Neil?

Those at the table made a convivial occasion of breakfast. As they ate, they heard the laughter of the other two little girls and Andrew, sledging in front of the house.

"Can I help you chop wood after breakfast?" Jamie asked eagerly. "You need a lot."

"You can help," Neil promised.

"Larry and I are going up to my room to listen to records," Ellie reported as the two of them finished their breakfast. Kathy was conscious of the air of pleased expectancy on Larry's face. "May we be excused?"

"Of course," Neil said gravely. He smiled as Kathy's eyes followed them out of the room. "Don't worry about Larry. He's doing fine."

"When will we chop the wood?" Jamie asked with strained patience as Kathy and Neil dallied over a second up of coffee.

"Right now." Neil grinned and pushed his chair back from the table. "After the size of the breakfast I've been stashing away, I'd better chop wood."

"Have another cup of coffee," Mrs McArdle urged Kathy. She came to the table with the percolator. "Nothing like fresh ground coffee with your breakfast."

"My third," Kathy laughed.

The phone rang. Mrs McArdle went to answer.

"Agnes, whatever happened to your voice?" she asked sympathetically after a moment. "Oh, laryngitis. Of course, I don't expect you to come in. Take plenty of tea and honey and stay in bed. Before you go to sleep tonight, slug down a shot of whisky. You'll be all right in the morning for sure." She listened, nodding slowly. "That's right. Now take care of yourself. We'll see you in the morning, God willing." She put down the phone, suddenly looked dismayed. "Oh, I clean forgot. Agnes was going to stop by the supermarket in town and bring me a bag of onions. I'll need them for tonight's stew. Oh well," she sighed, "I'll have to drive in and pick them up after lunch."

"I'll get the onions for you, Mrs McArdle," Kathy offered, then hesitated. "That is, if you don't mind keeping an eye on Larry."

"I don't mind at all." Pleased with this arrangement Mrs McArdle walked to the canister beside the sink, where petty cash for household needs was kept. "Take your time while you're in town. Park the car at the supermarket and walk around. See the town." She chuckled. "What there is of it."

Kathy paused.

"Perhaps I ought to go upstairs and ask Larry if he wants to go with me."

"He won't," Mrs McArdle prophesied. "He's having too good a time with Ellie."

Kathy went upstairs to Ellie's room. Larry and Ellie were deeply engrossed in listening to records.

"I want to stay with Ellie," he told Kathy.

She returned to the kitchen. Larry was enjoying being with the children, she thought with pleasure. He was not nearly as tense as he had been when they arrived.

"I'll give the children cookies and juice in about an hour or so," Mrs McArdle promised. "Don't worry about rushing back. Enjoy yourself."

Neil glanced up with a smile when she encountered him at the woodpile with Jamie. She explained her mission.

"Let me get the car out for you. It's rough to

manoeuvre out of the barn."

"Thanks." It was absurd to feel such pleasure because Neil smiled at her. *Stop this craziness.*

Kathy slid behind the wheel and swung down the driveway. The two girls and Andrew paused on their sledges at her exhortation. In the pen the geese were complaining noisily. As she drove onto the road, she heard Neil calling to them to shut up. He was about to let them out for the day.

Again she admired the splendour of the mountains that lay to her right and ahead of her. A countryside for artists. She drove with a sense of well-being — pleased that she had accepted this holiday season job.

Making a left at the light, she recalled Mrs McArdle's instructions. The supermarket was just down the street.

Randall allowed a pick-up truck to get between him and Kathy's car. No sweat. He could keep her in sight. He didn't want her to know he was trailing her.

He leaned forward as she paused at the light, which was turning green now. She was making a left into town. He'd swear she was alone, but he'd better be careful. Larry might be slouched down out of sight. Larry would recognise his voice in an instant.

The pick-up moved straight ahead. He turned left. Kathy was swinging onto the supermarket parking lot. He drove past it. Slowly so that he could see who emerged from Kathy's car. She was alone. The kid was up at the house. He was in luck.

Randall drove a block past the supermarket, made a U-turn and returned to park before it. He sauntered casually into the store. Kathy was already walking towards the check-out counter. OK, go buy a pack of cigarettes.

"Hi, fancing meeting you here!" he greeted her enthusiastically. "Have a good Christmas?"

"Busy with the kids at the school. How's the skiing?" Kathy's smile was warm.

"It's great. I'm out there by six." He paused. Grinned ingenuously. "How about taking pity on me again? My buddy's still tied up on the job, and I'm running around talking to myself. Have coffee with me at the diner across the way? I hear they have hot doughnuts to go with it."

"All right," she accepted. Avidly, he congratulated himself. She was bored with chasing after those kids. "As soon as I buy these." She held up a bag of onions.

"Let's get in line." He prodded her towards the check-out counter. "I have to pick up cigarettes." He only smoked when he was uptight. He took pride in keeping his body in perfect condition.

They waited behind a woman buying for a family of ten. Randall was impatient to be out of here and sitting across a table from Kathy. Working the Randall Brooks magic. Of course, to her he was Rick Jamison.

He'd invite Kathy to lunch in Manchester tomorrow. With Larry. Kathy and Larry would never make it to Manchester. He felt marvellous today. No headache. Clean mountain air in his lungs. And optimistic that by tomorrow night he would be in the car and headed back to New York.

Finally Kathy and Randall were out of the supermarket. They went first to Kathy's car so that she could put away the bag of onions. A friendly collie dog wandered over to be petted. Kathy fussed over it for a few moments until Randall, striving for a humorous approach, drew her away. To hell with the dog. He had to set up this lunch date for tomorrow.

They walked into the diner across the way. Randall piloted her to a rear table against the wall, where they were assured a certain amount of privacy.

"I won't spend another Christmas alone in a town like this," Randall said wryly and noticed the quick sympathy this elicited from Kathy. "My buddy was supposed to be up here for sure. But he works for his father. I think the family's deliberately tying him up. Me, I'm a loner." He shrugged this off, began to improvise. "My folks kicked off when I was a kid. I was raised by an older sister who lives down in Peru now. Too long a haul for Christmas — and too expensive. Besides, wherever there's a ski slope is home to me." She was sopping it all up.

"I've never ski'd," Kathy confessed. "One of these winters I'll give it a whirl."

"Any time you'd like to go out on the slopes,

give me the word," he said, then leaned back as a waitress came over to take their orders.

"Skiing is an expensive deal." Kathy was candid. "I won't invest this year."

"You can rent equipment," he pointed out.

"I'll wait," she laughed.

"I mean to go over to ski in Manchester before I leave. I hear that's a sensational town. You drive down the highway, right through town; and the mountains rise on both sides of you. Some terrific restaurants, too, though I hear you have to watch out for the ones that demand a month's salary for lunch. What about lunch in Manchester tomorrow?" He made it sound an inspiration of the moment. "At a place that won't take a month's salary. It's just twenty-three miles from Salem."

"I don't know what I'm doing tomorrow," she explained, seeming startled at his suggestion. "I mean, I have to plan around Larry."

"Bring the kid along." He was intent on being ingratiating. "He won't be any trouble."

"If you're sure . . ." Kathy was ambivalent.

"I'm sure," he said firmly. "Oh, there's just one problem," he said apologetically. His mind racing ahead. "I have to hang around the motel in the morning in case Norman calls. Could you drive over to my motel, leave your car there, and then the three of us will drive to Manchester in mine?"

"Sure," Kathy agreed. She liked the idea of lunch in Manchester — with the kid along so he shouldn't get any ideas, Randall interpreted. "When shall we pick you up?"

"Is noon all right?" *She bit. It was going to work out.*

"Noon's fine."

She wanted to spend some time away from the school. She was bored out of her skull hanging around there, he told himself with satisfaction. OK. After tomorrow she wouldn't have to stay at the school any longer.

She could accompany the body back to New York.

Chapter Twenty-One

Mrs McArdle gazed at Kathy in astonishment.

"No breakfast this morning?" she reproached. "Are you coming down with a virus?"

"I'll have a couple of those gorgeous biscuits and some coffee," Kathy said apologetically. She was conscious of Neil's look of solicitude. "I'm having an early lunch in Manchester." She forced a smile. "Larry's coming along." She didn't say with whom she was having lunch. Already she regretted making the date. She'd accepted because she was unnerved by the way she felt about Neil.

"I'm taking the kids over to sledge at that hill down the road," Neil told her. "We'll take along hot chocolate and sandwiches for lunch. I figure we'll make a day of it."

His eyes revealed his disappointment that she wouldn't be going with them. Did he suspect she was having lunch with Rick? She was having lunch with Rick to make Neil understand he must not push this too fast. It terrified her to comprehend how emotionally involved she was with Neil. In such a short span of time.

"I don't think Larry would go sledging." Why did she feel so guilty at having lunch with Rick? She had made no commitment to Neil. They hardly knew each other. "I'm afraid he'd be scared."

"He might not with Ellie," Neil said. "They've struck up a beautiful friendship."

"I'll ask Larry later," Kathy compromised. Right now they could hear the laughter of the children in the living room as they played a word game. But she was fairly certain Larry would be fearful of sledging.

Kathy and Neil lingered over coffee. Their conversation was bright but impersonal despite a strong personal undercurrent. They were still at the table when Agnes pulled up behind the house in her ancient Volvo and came into the kitchen. Clearly excited about something.

"I woulda been here earlier," she said, "but I had to stop to see what was happening when I was driving out of Rupert." Kathy remembered that Agnes lived across the state line, in Vermont. "The State Police caught a pair of hunters in clear daylight. Stashing away a deer in the back of their station wagon. Boy, did they lace into those characters! Everybody knows deer are out of season. They'll be lucky if they draw less than ninety days in the clink."

Kathy and Neil exchanged a swift, comprehending glance.

"They must have been the ones who were poaching in our woods." Neil sighed in relief. "We won't have to worry about that anymore. I was sure it couldn't be local people."

"Are you still taking the kids to sledge down the road?" Kathy suspected he had dreamt up that project to keep them off the pond.

"Why not?" He smiled indulgently. "It's a great hill for sledging. Better than anything on the property here. And it'll give them a change of scenery."

"Maybe I can persuade Larry to give it a try after lunch."

It would be fun to have lunch in Manchester with Rick, she encouraged herself. Maybe it would help to push away the memory of that close call up there on the pond. And Larry would be with her. Otherwise, she wouldn't be having lunch with Rick. Instinct warned her that Rick would come on strong with little provocation.

Was the hunter Larry and she encountered one of the group in Rupert? Neil seemed to think so. Yet some inner intuition told her that this wasn't so. Hunters after deer wouldn't bother with a squirrel.

Chapter Twenty-Two

Randall saw Chris as he fastened his skis on top of the car. He had figured on avoiding her this morning. He had business to transact.

"Rick!" she yelled shrilly. "You leaving already?"

"I have to meet a buddy coming up from the city," he lied. "He's just passing through on his way to Quebec City."

"I rushed over to see you," she sulked. "Do you have to go right now?" Her eyes were blatantly inviting.

"We could stop somewhere for coffee," he said. But he was already plotting another destination. There was time. She was a cow, but she was better than nothing. She thought he was sensational. "Follow me in your car, Chris."

He slid behind the wheel of his car, went through the routine problem of getting the motor to turn over. He drove half a mile, with Chris tailgating, before he pulled off at the side of the road where flanking tall evergreens had suffered a devastating blight.

Randall left the car, went to the boot, lifted the door. The rifle was in his motel unit. He'd pick it up later. He reached for the blanket and brought it out. He waited while Chris drew up behind him and climbed out of her car.

"Get in the back seat," he said tersely, pointing to his car.

Her eyes opened wide in disbelief.

"Rick, are you crazy? Right here on the road?"

"Nobody comes this way," he said carelessly. "Besides, we've got a blanket. Who's stopping to look inside the car?"

They settled themselves on the back seat. The blanket provided meagre camouflage. Randall wasted little time on preliminaries today. Why the hell did she have to giggle? Anita used to swear like a marine. That he'd enjoyed. He knew just what to do to make Anita climb the walls. Damn Anita!

"Rick!" Chris stiffened beneath him. "Stop pulling my hair."

"Baby, I'm sorry," He pulled his hands away from her hair, moved them to caress her back. "I got carried away." He used to pull his kid sister's hair that way until she screamed. Mom carried on like crazy. "Come on, Chris! Let's get this show on the road!"

"Can't we at least go in for coffee?" Chris pouted, pulling on her parka again. "You don't know that your friend's at the motel yet."

"We'll have coffee tomorrow," Randall promised. Tomorrow, if he played today right, he'd be on his way into New York. He could shack up a few nights with the publicity gal from the Hamptons. She was holding his gear for him, anyway.

"You treat me awful," Chris scolded. "I don't know why I bother with you."

"You know why." His eyes were smug. "OK, beat it. I have to drive back to the motel."

He waited until Chris had pulled out of the road, then followed her until his turn-off. He carefully watched the time. In half an hour Kathy — with Larry — ought to be approaching the motel. He'd station himself on the road ten minutes earlier, just in case she arrived ahead of time. *Don't strike out this time.*

He parked in front of his motel unit and let himself inside with the key. The room had been made up in his absence, but the girl wouldn't know about the rifle hidden on the shelf beneath the wool shirts he'd piled up there. Even if she was the curious type and poked around, she'd figure he'd hid it lest somebody steal it. This was hunting season. It wouldn't look suspicious that he carried a rifle with him.

Randall reached up on the shelf to bring down the rifle. One at a time he injected the bullets into the magazine. Only four, but he wouldn't need more than one. Two — if Kathy saw him.

He laid the rifle across the bed. A cold excitement gripped him. In his mind he visualised Anita's face when they called to tell her Larry was dead. Her hold on the trust fund would be forever gone. The money would go to that museum.

She wouldn't be beautiful at the cemetery. He would be there to watch her crying. She'd blame herself for sending Larry up to the school for the holidays. Her fault that her kid was dead, and the money gone. Nobody but herself to blame.

Nobody would ever know he stood right at the side of the road, concealed by the bushes, and put a bullet through Larry's head. He could do that with no sweat.

He looked at his watch. OK, leave now. The hunting licence pinned to the back of his jacket, the way it was supposed to be. Nobody would bother to come close enough to see that the licence was issued to Randall Brooks, while he was registered here as Rick Jamison. He would be just another hunter on the track of small game. He chuckled. Larry was small game, but the pay-off was the greatest.

He left his room, walked across the parking area into the woods. Moving south with purposeful strides. Knowing his destination. Move parallel to the road, he instructed himself, for about a hundred yards. Take up his position behind a bush with a clear view of the road.

He settled on a spot, stripped off his gloves and shoved them into his pocket. Now he stood with the rifle in readiness. Plenty of time to bring it into position, look into the sight. All the hours he had spent on the range would pay off today.

The minutes dragged. His hands ached with the cold. But he wasn't worried about his accuracy. He was trained for this mission. Unknowingly he had trained himself. She ought to show up soon. She wouldn't stand him up, would she? Nobody stood up Randall Brooks.

His mind raced backward. Remember that little bitch, five feet tall and ninety pounds soaking wet, who gave him a hard time his first year at college? She broke a date with him to go to a bash with some big wheel on campus.

He was waiting outside with a knife in his hand when she came out with the guy. He wasn't going to cut her up. He just wanted to scare the hell out of her. He was too smart to let himself get caught cutting up a chick. Right away, he let the guy know he was just bluffing. But if she had been alone on a dark street, he might have sunk that knife right into her heart, up to the handle.

Randall straightened up. He spied the car. Her car. With the right licence number. Kathy and the kid. He lifted the rifle to his shoulder. His heart pounded. Don't miss.

His fingers reached for the trigger as the car moved into range. Get him on the sight. *Shoot!*

Chapter Twenty-Three

Randall's trigger finger froze. Where was Larry? Had he slid down into the seat until he was out of sight? Hadn't Kathy brought him with her?

He snapped into action, charged through the woods towards the motel. Hell, she'd be there ahead of him! Breathlessly he arrived at the rear of his unit, hastily dug into the snow to bury the rifle. He'd have to pick it up later. It would be safe here.

He circled around to come out of the woods into the parking area. Her car sat in front of the office. He crossed to the entrance. Kathy was inside asking for him. She was alone. The hunting licence! Take it off his jacket quick. Wrong name.

He pulled open the door of the office, contrived a convivial smile.

"Hi, Kathy."

She spun around to face him. Her smile warm.

"I thought I'd missed you. You weren't answering your phone."

"I was hiking through the woods. You don't get this kind of air down in the city. I didn't realise it was so late," he apologised.

"Actually, I'm a few minutes early."

The motel manager figured he was taking her into the sack. Surprise. Let him see them drive off. Maybe later, he decided, he'd ask her to come back to his room. Maybe he needed to get closer to her to nail the kid. Damn! He had been sure this was going to be it.

Randall concentrated on being charming. Kathy was tense. Was she worried about having lunch with him and leaving Larry behind?

"How's the little boy doing?" he asked with a show of polite interest while they settled themselves in his car.

"I think he's enjoying himself up here." Kathy seemed pleased. "I invited him to come along with me, but at the last minute his friend Ellie persuaded him to go with the other children on an outing."

"Outing?"

"They're going sledging down the road where there's a perfect steep hill. They're taking along a picnic, and they'll have hot chocolate from a thermos. It's a big deal," she laughed.

"I'll cut over to Highway 153," he said casually as they moved out on to the road. So she had meant to bring Larry with her. Damn the brat for changing his mind! "I hear it's the most picturesque route to Manchester. We go right through Dorset, too."

He leaned forward to switch on the radio. He moved the dial till he found a programme he liked. Kathy's eyes were skimming the scenery. They passed vast sweeps of open fields. Here and there was a century-old farmhouse. Mountains rose in the distance — a symphony in white and black. Winter-dark trees were silhouetted against the sky like masses of delicate filigree.

"I never knew there were so many cows," Kathy laughed. Her eyes focused on a herd of cows heavy with milk.

"We're crossing into Vermont now." Randall pointed to a marker at the railroad crossing. "See?"

He drove through the town of Rupert. Where was the sign that pointed to Manchester? There it was.

"We're going around the side of a mountain, aren't we?" Kathy asked curiously. The mountain was snow-encrusted, with gaunt trees rising like porcupine quills.

"That's right. Disappointed in the views?" he jibed. Hell, how was he supposed to nail the kid? *The days were running by too fast.* After the fiasco on Christmas Day he was uneasy about approaching the house again. Larry should have come along today. It would have been all over by now.

"The scenery is magnificent," Kathy said enthusiastically. "Look at the sun, resting on the valley there. Isn't it fantastic?"

They followed Route 30 into Dorset, past rows of white houses. An endless array of white houses. Snowmobiles zoomed over snow-covered fields on their left. At intervals antique shops lined the road.

They drove through Dorset, following the signs to Manchester.

"I hear there's great deli right off the main part

142

of town," Randall reported. "Shall we give it a whirl?" His eyes were admiring as they rested on her for a moment.

"Why not?" she agreed lightly.

In Manchester they turned off the main street as the motel manager had directed. They paused before the entrance road to a cluster of red, white-trimmed, artistic-appearing shops.

"No place to park in there," Randall noted, frowning in annoyance.

"Try next door," Kathy urged. "In front of the supermarket."

They circled the parking area before the super-market three times before someone relinquished a wedge of parking space.

"Everybody's up for the skiing," Kathy sur-mised. "This is one of the big winter weekends."

They left the car and walked across to the clus-ter of shops. The deli was towards the rear. Ran-dall opened the door. They inched their way into the crowded store. The tables to the left, the counter space at right angles to the tables jammed with sportswear-clad patrons. A line waited be-fore the serving counter.

"It's self-service," Randall realised in surprise. "Hell, we'll have to wait forever!" But he didn't want to go to one of those fancy restaurants that would set him back a fortune. His eyes moved speculatively about the room. The deli sold gour-met items, a variety of cheeses. Bottles of wine lined the far shelves; notices advised that this must not be consumed on the premises. "Hey,

I've got an idea." Charm spilled over from him again. "Why don't we buy some cheese, a bread, a bottle of wine, and picnic in the car? I'm sure they'll sell us paper cups."

"Great," Kathy approved. "I love cheese and wine."

Randall's eyes skimmed the area behind the counter.

"They've got pecan pie. Do you like it?"

"I love it. With whipped cream." She pointed to wedges of pecan pie topped with whipped cream that were being passed over the counter.

They chose their cheeses, debated about the wine. Anita had taught him about wine, Randall reminded himself smugly. Anita had been a liberal education. He chose with an air of authority that was meant to impress Kathy.

With the spoils of their shopping they returned to the car. They drove until they discovered a spot along the road that pleased them and parked.

"You can't beat a view like this," Randall said with satisfaction while they prepared a makeshift dinner table between them on the front seat of the car. "The mountains rising on both sides this way. The fields covered with snow. I'm sorry I didn't bring along my camera. I've got a sensational Nikon." Anita had a Nikon. "I'd love to get some shots of this." How could he set up another deal like today, where he could be sure she'd bring the kid along? He'd have to dig around for an angle.

"There goes another bunch of hunters." Kathy

144

shuddered in distaste. Randall followed her gaze to a car that had just pulled off the road a hundred fifty feet or so ahead of them, disgorging red-capped hunters with rifles. "I hope they're not after deer."

"It's out of season for deer," he said automatically. His mind was working on another level. How did he get the kid set up again? Maybe there was some special holiday season entertainment for kids over at Saratoga or Bennington. Somewhere close. Check it out. *He had to get the kid off the road.*

"Some hunters don't care whether it's the season or not," Kathy said wryly. "The State Police picked up a pair of men this morning over near Rupert. They'd just bagged a deer. It didn't mean a thing to them that it was out of season." Her eyes held a glow of anger. "Probably the same hunters who came through our woods on Christmas Day and shot a squirrel right at the pond. They just missed hitting Larry or me."

"Good Lord!" Randall credibly professed shock. "Well, you won't have to worry about them anymore."

All at once Randall was charged with satisfaction. They were not scared of poachers any more. They thought the guys with the deer had been shooting on the school grounds. Terrific! He wouldn't have to worry about moving through their woods. They wouldn't be on the watch for hunters.

When he hit the kid, he'd have plenty of time

to cut out because they were not expecting any more trouble like that. And they'd think it was another crazy hunter from the city.

He was back in business. Right on home territory. Just the way he had planned it.

Chapter Twenty-Four

Kathy sat in a rocker before the Franklin stove in the kitchen. An open book across her lap. She had abandoned reading after the first page to gaze into the satin redness of the logs that burned in the grate. At regular intervals her eyes strayed to the clock. Neil was making a day of it with the children.

She had enjoyed the time with Rick because she knew this was just a casual encounter. Seeing Manchester had been fun. But when Rick had suggested a drive over to Saratoga tomorrow, she had manufactured a busy schedule. That was a relationship she had no intention of pursuing.

What was she going to do about Neil? He was falling in love with her, wasn't he? As surely as she was falling in love with him. But how could she be sure that it was real? They were up here at a magical time of the year.

She liked so much about Neil. She could visualise herself being married to him. It was never that way with Clint. She would never have married Clint, even if he had asked her — not when she'd thought the situation through clearly. She had met Clint when she was lonely, shaken by her parents' death. Clint had been a crutch to see her through a rough period.

Neil had such beautiful tenderness with the

children. He was so dedicated to his work. She could see herself involved in the kind of life Neil would forge for himself.

She had gone out with Rick today because she was running from Neil. Neil evoked visions of a permanent commitment. Was Neil thinking that way? He talked to her about coming down to New York in February. Seeing her. Too fast, she told herself again. This was happening too fast.

Mrs McArdle moved about the house pulling down shades. Dusk came so early this time of year. Mrs McArdle pulled down the shades to keep in the heat. It was a way of saving on oil bills.

"Here they come now," Mrs McArdle called from a window at the front of the living room. "Just listen to them carrying on," she chuckled. "They must have had a high old time."

In minutes the kitchen ricocheted with the sounds of children's voices as they struggled out of boots, discarded jackets and snow-encrusted caps.

"All right, everybody." Mrs McArdle was firm. "Line up your boots over there near the radiator. Put your jackets in your rooms. And change your trousers, too," she admonished. "I'll bet you're all soaking wet. Out in the snow all these hours."

Kathy watched while Larry removed his own boots, took off his jacket, confidently reached out a hand to Ellie so that he could be guided back to his room.

"Larry's doing well up here," Neil said quietly,

following Kathy's gaze. "I'm glad Ellie and he hit it off this way. It's good for Ellie, too. She came here last year with severe reading and spelling difficulties, though she tested out as well above average in intelligence. We finally decided on a method of teaching, and she's reading almost at grade level. But we'd been worried about a set-back because of her not being able to go home for Christmas when she'd looked forward to that." He smiled. "Larry's helping her through the season."

"Mrs Cantrell ought to arrange training for Larry — to cope with his blindness, I mean." Kathy was sombre. "She told me that the tutor reads the lessons to Larry, and he listens to them on a tape recorder until they're absorbed. But that's only a stop-gap measure."

"Did you have a good day?" Neil asked unexpectedly.

"I loved Manchester," she parried. "Those magnificent old houses. And the mountains everywhere."

"Mrs McArdle offered to keep an eye on the children if we wanted to go out to dinner tonight." Neil's voice was casual, but his eyes were eager. "She figured we might be in the mood for a change of scenery. Would you like to go?"

Mrs McArdle was reading romance in the air, Kathy thought indulgently. But Neil and she owed themselves a chance to test out their emotions. Yet she was ambivalent.

"I feel guilty leaving Larry alone again —"

"It's good for him to see that he can function without you," Neil said confidently. "He did fine this afternoon. Had a ball. Let's have dinner over at the Log Cabin. It's not fancy, but the food's good and they serve plenty of it." He chuckled reminiscently. "Even I feel like carrying a doggie bag away from there. And there's a fireplace going all the time."

"I know." Kathy's smile was dazzling. "I was at the Log Cabin for coffee." She didn't say she was there with Rick, but Neil guessed. "I'd love to have dinner there with you."

Early — slightly past six — with the children seated comfortably about the table in the dining room while Mrs McArdle prepared to serve, Kathy and Neil left in the van.

As they drove towards the Log Cabin, Neil talked about school problems.

"We have one little boy — he's seven now — as a day student. His parents drive fifty miles each way to bring him to us, and this is his second year. But we're getting through to him," he said with satisfaction. "He was apparently normal up to eighteen months. Then, for no reason his parents could figure out, he stopped talking. He had an obsession to hide at regular intervals. When the weather was warm, he would run out and hide among the bushes. Then the weather turned cold, and we found him hiding in the geese house. We dug up a huge paper carton, brought it into the house, covered it with a throw rug as a curtain — and he has a fine place to hide now. He's beginning to talk a bit. Not regularly and not often — but just before the holidays he talked to me after he'd finished a puzzle the other kids couldn't put together. He glowed."

Listening to Neil, Kathy felt a beautiful closeness to him. She was sorry that the discussion was interrupted by their arrival at the restaurant. Emerging from the car they sniffed the pungent scent of burning wood. As they left the car to walk to the entrance, they saw the Christmas tree through the wide expanse of window, drapes pulled open tonight.

Despite the early hour the restaurant was filling. They found a table for two close to the fireplace, where logs were piled high in the grate. A fat orange candle on the table burnt in welcome.

Tonight the moments of horror on the pond seemed light years past. Yet her mind insisted on focusing on those moments. Dissecting them. It was paranoid of her to try to link that with the incident on the Taconic. Who in this world would want to kill her?

Kathy and Neil both ordered the roast beef dinner. Kathy was wide-eyed when she saw the gigantic portions.

"I'll never be able to eat all this!" she laughed.

"Do your best." Neil grinned. "We'll take what you don't eat home in a doggie bag for the geese. They're beginning to think they're people."

Not until they were at dessert did the conversation lose its dinner table lightness.

"Kathy, you're going to be up here for such a

short while," Neil said seriously. "I have to tell you before you go back to New York. I want to see a lot of you. I'm in love with you, Kathy."

"Neil, we hardly know each other." But her heart pounded in exhilaration. "Please, don't let's rush too far ahead."

"I won't rush you," he promised. "I'll come down to New York in February. You'll come up here for the spring holidays. Kathy, I'm talking about a permanent commitment."

"I've never been so drawn to anyone in my life," she said with candour. This was a moment that demanded honesty. "But I've had a bad experience. Just a little while ago. I must be sure."

"You'll be sure," Neil promised, and reached out a hand to cover hers. "Let's just give ourselves a chance."

Chapter Twenty-Five

Randall stirred restlessly in his chair at the small table in the rear of the bar. The room was deeply shadowed, murky with cigar smoke from a patron at the next table. The jukebox was an endless raucous shriek.

Business was slow. At regular intervals Chris came over to talk to him. He was drinking too many beers. Tomorrow he'd feel lousy.

Chris emerged from behind the bar to slide in the chair across from him.

"Hang around another hour," Chris coaxed. "When it's this slow, the old man lets me leave early. We can go somewhere." Her eyes were bright in invitation.

"I've got a bitch of a headache," he hedged. "I'm going back to the motel in a few minutes."

"Want an aspirin?"

"No." He was brusque. He had the pills back at the motel, but he couldn't take them on top of all those beers. Besides, the pills slowed him down. He had to be alert now. He couldn't afford any more slip-ups. He had a job to do. He had retrieved the rifle; it was back on the shelf of his closet in the motel room. Ready for action.

"You going to be on the slopes tomorrow?" Her smile said she expected an affirmative answer.

"No," he said sharply. "I'm sleeping late to-morrow."

"Maybe you can go with me to look at that Honda before I come to work tomorrow." She leaned forward so that she all but spilled out of her low-cut blouse. "I can pick it up dirt cheap, but I'm scared I'll get screwed on the deal. I don't know the first thing about Hondas."

"I bought one the summer I was seventeen. I drove it all the way out to California, and then it fell apart." He shrugged. "Get somebody who knows more about them to check it out for you." He pushed back his chair. "I'm going to beat it, Chris. See you around."

He left the bar knowing she was furious. He enjoyed her rage. Cheap little slut. Anita was an expensive little slut. And he was giving her an expensive Christmas present.

Snow was beginning to fall as he slid behind the wheel of the car. While he drove along the near-empty roads, the flakes came down heavier. If this kept up, the gritters would be out on the roads by morning. No skiing tomorrow, he sur-mised. Not for anybody. For himself it would be a solid night's sleep and into action.

Chris was teed off because he'd refused to go with her to look at that Honda. He had been royally screwed on the one he bought after high school graduation. They were living in a suburb of Cleveland that year. Christ, he had been bored in that town. Bored in high school. He had spent most of his time conked out in front of a TV set.

At seventeen he had looked like twenty. That was the year he walked around with the beard and the long hair. He bought the Honda, left a note in the kitchen for Mom, and cut out for California. With his build, his way with chicks, he should have been a natural for a TV series.

That damn Honda conked out right on Sunset Boulevard. He knew it was no use trying to have it fixed. He had forty bucks on him and no job in sight. He left the Honda right there on the Boulevard and walked away.

He smiled with sardonic humour. Two nights later he met Maggie. What a character! She must have been fifty-six if she was a day, and hotter than sixteen in the sack. Maggie called herself an actors' agent. What a line she threw him about getting him into TV!

Maggie bought him some decent clothes, put him up in her apartment. She liked making the scene with a young stud. They were a pair when they went out. He in his skintight suede suit and Maggie gussied up like something out of a studio wardrobe department, circa 1920. She went big for spangled dresses cut down to her belly-button, and she needed a derrick to hold up her boobs. It was Maggie who taught him the esoteric angles in sex.

"Look, baby," she'd drawled, staring at him through inch-long false eyelashes, "there's the dull, old-fashioned way, and there are the fancy ones. You hang around Maggie, and you'll become a master."

He waited four months for the old slut to land him a part in a TV series.

"Baby, what's the matter?" she'd reproach him when he blew his stack over the delay. "You don't become a TV star overnight. You've got to work first." He worked plenty. Sometimes three or four times a night. Where did that old bitch get the stamina?

Then she came to him one night with a sassy grin on her face.

"Baby, I have a part for you," she chortled, putting her unexpectedly small, fat hands on his chest.

"In a pilot film?" He'd tingled with excitement.

"Not exactly," she explained. "It's the lead in this movie short. They start work in the morning."

He was flying high until she told him what he had to do. He was the stag in a stag movie. He ripped her clothes off and beat her to a pulp. Then he called for an ambulance.

Maggie didn't dare identify him to the cops. She was booking talent for a stag movie. She gave the cops some cock-and-bull story about an intruder with a stocking over his face. Did they ever shoot that movie? Probably. Plenty of hungry guys wandered about Hollywood. He hadn't been that hungry.

Randall pulled up before the motel, dark except for the lighted 'Vacancy' sign. He'd take a pill and hit the sack. Should he set the alarm? No, he'd wake in good time. Nobody budged from that house before ten in the morning. He would be there in plenty of time for the action.

He left the car and let himself into his unit. He debated a moment, then switched on the colour TV. He stripped down to shorts and inspected himself in the mirror. He should have hung around California. He might have made it in TV.

Maybe he would head out that way again. Once Anita got what was coming to her. Or he might jet down to Rio. He'd saved plenty those months he'd worked for Anita, plus he had his severance pay.

He took the pill and stretched out on the bed. He was too uptight to sleep. Give the pill a chance to go to work. He flipped through the magazines in the rack. Nothing worth looking at — and nothing he wanted to see on the box.

Go to sleep. The pill would start working in a few minutes. He needed a steady hand tomorrow. He leaned over to turn off the lamp, pulled the covers up, and leaned back against the pillows. Already his headache was letting up.

Tomorrow was going to be lucky for him, he decided in fresh optimism. He had that crazy feeling that everything would work out right on schedule. He could almost feel the rifle in his hand. He could hear the bullet whistling through the air. Larry wouldn't have a chance.

Chapter Twenty-Six

Randall woke up with a rotten taste in his mouth. A drugged feeling. That was what happened when he slept a long time, he told himself in exasperation. Four or five hours was all he needed.

He pulled himself up in bed. His eyes sought the calendar. Time was breathing down his neck. He had to do it today. *Why was it so hard to knock off that stupid kid?*

Anybody could walk up and put a bullet through Larry's head. That wasn't the smart way to do it. You played it sharp so you didn't get caught.

From now on all he did was stalk Larry. Four more days and they'd be heading back for New York unless he pulled off this job. All at once he felt good. He'd do it. Just like he'd planned. In a way that nobody could pin on him.

He dressed, brought the rifle down from the shelf, and carried it out to the car. The rifle neatly concealed in the blanket. He left the motel and headed for the restaurant at the shopping centre for breakfast. He'd buy himself a red and black chequered jacket. Like half the guys around here wore. The shearling jacket was a trademark.

Today he'd leave the shearling jacket in the car. He had ski goggles in the glove compartment. Wear the ski cap and goggles, just in case somebody spotted him. Nobody would know him from a man from outer space in that get-up.

At the restaurant he ordered a hearty breakfast. Pancakes, sausages, a side order of home fries.

"Keep the coffee coming," he ordered the waitress.

He ate with relish. Despite his drugged feeling on awakening, he was alert now. No headache. A man with a mission. He paid his bill, tipped heavily, sauntered from the restaurant into the huge sprawling store where he had bought the bullets on Tuesday.

He made his way back to the men's department and found the identical jacket he had seen on a dozen men in the past four days. He tried it on, visualising himself in the goggles and ski cap. Nobody would recognize him.

He left the store. In the car he changed into the chequered jacket and threw the shearling jacket into the back. OK, head for Salem now.

He'd drive by the house before he tried to go up into the woods, he plotted. He had to make sure those damn geese were out front. He didn't want to announce his arrival.

Approaching the house, he skimmed the scenery. It was hard to see the geese against all that snow. Then suddenly the air was assaulted by vigorous squawking. They were still in the pen. Complaining about it.

He'd have to drive around a while. Wait until the geese were let loose. But as he drove past the house, he heard the sound of a young boy's high voice above their noise.

"OK, shut up! I'm coming! I'm coming!"

The boy would let them out. Great! Drive down the road. Cut off onto that side road and park along the open fields. Then walk across the road and climb up into the woods at the rear of the property. Go to the old barn. Stay there. Watch. There had to come a moment when he could pull this off.

Before he left the car, he pulled the ski cap protectively low about his face and put on the goggles. He looked up and down the road. Not a human being in sight. The rifle in one hand, he left the car and walked towards his destination.

Moving through the protective covering of multi-acred woods, he heard the sounds of the children's voices in the house below. He stalked ahead with a sense of being in command. He travelled far above the pond, but he still had a clear view of the house below.

Stay up here, he revised his plan on instinct. Don't go down to the old barn. It was safer here. He had a sensational view of the house. It was a matter of time. Sooner or later Larry would show up. All he needed was a minute. One minute. One bullet.

The weather was sharp. Too cold to stand still. He'd better walk up and down before his feet froze. No need to worry about anybody being on the prowl for trespassers. Down at the house everybody was sure the trespassers had been caught.

160

Up here he was like a king on top of a mountain. In control.

The drab overcast sky gave way to sun in a matter of minutes, but in the near-zero weather this did little for his comfort. He waited with growing impatience for some sign of Larry and Kathy. Walking back and forth over the snow-blanketed earth, he beat a path forty feet long.

Randall stiffened to attention. A cluster of children was emerging from the house in the company of a man. Four kids, he counted. They were walking up the incline towards the pond. Swinging ice-skates from their hands. He retreated. He still had a clear view of what was happening below.

Larry wasn't with them. It would be too risky, anyhow, to try to pick him off with the others skating on the pond. If he hit Larry, one crazy kid might come tearing after him. *No stupid mistakes today.*

He took up a position on a small plateau. His eyes swept the dramatic panorama. All of Salem on display plus the surrounding towns extending miles away. How long were those brats going to stay on the pond? Where were Larry and Kathy?

The children and the man with them skated amid steady bursts of hilarity. Randall watched in growing irritation. Maybe when the others returned to the house, Kathy would bring Larry up to the pond. The two of them had skated alone on Christmas Day.

While Randall swore under his breath at this

delay, the others skated until the man ordered them to take off their skates and head back to the house.

"You've been in the cold long enough. This weather is raw." The man's voice was good-humoured but firm. "Let's get back to the house."

With the others gone Randall moved with more freedom. Damn, his feet were numb from tramping over the snow all this time. His hands were stiff inside his gloves. But not too stiff to shoot with accuracy.

He checked his watch. He had been up here over an hour. Why in hell hadn't he thought to buy a thermos and bring along hot coffee?

Now he froze at attention. Voices below. With a sense of anticipation he moved to a better position. Kathy had come out of the house with Larry and a little girl. They were coming up towards the woods. So there was another kid with them. He had to take the chance.

Randall stripped off his gloves. He lifted the rifle to his shoulder, squinted through the sight. The kids were hopping about too much. He couldn't hit a moving target at this distance.

All right. Wait. There would be one second when Larry and the other kid would pause. Larry would be on target. *Wait for that second.*

Exultation charged through him. This time Anita would get her Christmas present.

Chapter Twenty-Seven

Zipping her jacket high about her throat, Kathy followed Larry and Ellie. They wouldn't stay out too long in this raw chill, but Larry and Ellie had been so intrigued by Mrs McArdle's story of antique bottles and unexpected treasures to be found in the dump — somewhere up in the woods — that she had allowed them to coax her into a search party. It was fantastic to realise that the dump had been used by the residents of the house over a hundred and forty years ago.

"Don't run too far ahead of me," Kathy called out. Enjoying their enthusiasm. Larry seemed unafraid with Ellie close to him. His hand was in Ellie's and he was prepared to go anywhere.

"Which way, Kathy?" Approaching the pond, Ellie halted in doubt.

"Mrs McArdle said that it's above the pond," Kathy reminded them. "We'll go up into the woods and start walking over towards the left." That was the area Mrs McArdle had indicated.

An earlier owner, Mrs McArdle said, had decorated the kitchen with antique bottles dug out of the dump. Larry had clamoured to go up there, even though he couldn't see, because Ellie was so eager to go.

Clinging to each other Larry and Ellie moved with youthful confidence through the barren trees. Pushing past clumps of underbrush here and there, giggling with pleasure at this unexpected adventure.

"Oh, there's a bunny!" Ellie cried out in delight. "Larry, he's a baby. He's so cute."

"Did he run away?" Larry asked.

"He wasn't going to hang around to talk to us." Ellie laughed in high spirits.

Kathy heard a snap of twigs somewhere in the woods. Lots of animals around, she thought. And suddenly she halted. That was a sneeze. Somebody just sneezed. A human being. Not an animal.

Fearful of what she would see, Kathy swung around to search the woods to their right. Alarm rippled through her. A man in a red and black chequered jacket, a rifle in his hand, was disappearing into the underbrush. What was he doing here? The 'No Hunting' signs were everywhere.

"Larry, Ellie, let's see how quickly we can reach the dump," she said urgently. "Let's move. Over that way." She pointed for Ellie's benefit, and Ellie drew Larry along with her.

The man didn't want them to see him. Because he was hunting on posted land? Or because he was hunting her? As they moved away, she heard another sneeze. *He wasn't running away. He was following them.* Hiding behind clumps of bushes, but she saw a protruding elbow.

She mustn't scream. He would shoot before Neil could rush from the house. She couldn't pick up Larry and Ellie and run.

"Let's see if we can walk faster . . ." She struggled to keep fear out of her voice as she looked over her shoulder. She caught one fast glimpse of the red and black chequered jacket. Unmistakably someone was stalking them. "Down this way," she ordered. Pointing below.

"But that goes back to the house," Ellie protested.

"I think I made a mistake," she fabricated. "Mrs McArdle meant for us to go towards the other side into those woods there."

Move out of the woods, then coax the children into a race for the house. With Ellie holding his hand Larry would run.

Kathy spied a clearing just below. A clearing would make them sitting ducks, her mind warned.

"There's the dump!" Ellie shrieked, realising this before Kathy did. "What are those boys doing there?"

Three husky teenagers were digging avidly in the dump. A shopping bag at one side was loaded with dirt-covered objects. Kathy took a deep sigh of relief. Thank God for these trespassers!

"Hi," she called out with shaky brightness. "Find anything interesting?"

The boys looked up with a start. Guilt written across their faces. They knew they were trespassing on private property. But bless them for trespassing today.

"Just some junk," the tallest of the three, heavily bearded but with a face that said he was no more than fifteen, explained awkwardly. "We figured nobody would care. . ." He paused nervously, turned to the other two for help.

"Nothin' real good," the short, stocky one said with an ingratiating grin. "You want us to put it back?"

"No, of course not. Not this time," she amended because they were trespassing. "On one condition," she stipulated, her air of levity panic-brushed. "The three of you come down to the house with us and have hot apple cider. You must be freezing to death, digging in there without gloves."

The three boys brightened.

"Yes'm, it's pretty cold," the youngest of the three — surely no more than thirteen but built like a man — acknowledged. "We'd sure appreciate hot apple cider."

"Can't we stay and look in the dump?" Ellie was outraged at the prospect of imminent departure. "We came up here to look for hidden treasure."

"We've located it, Ellie," Kathy soothed. "That's enough for today. Tomorrow we'll come up and dig. It's awfully cold. I don't want you two getting sick. We'll all go down to the house and have something hot to drink."

He wouldn't dare follow the six of them, Kathy reasoned. Still, she encouraged the others to move quickly. Casting nervous glances over her shoulder at irregular intervals. The two men who had killed the deer over near Rupert were other

166

trespassers. They had a special trespasser all of their own. And he wasn't after deer.

At the house Mrs McArdle politely masked her astonishment at the guests Kathy had brought along. She served hot apple cider and doughnuts just out of the deep-fryer to a most appreciative trio.

In the living room Kathy reported to Neil about the incident on the plateau.

"I know it sounds crazy, but I'm sure he was stalking us. First he hid behind the bushes. Then he got bolder and moved in closer." She shuddered in recall. "I don't know what would have happened if we hadn't stumbled onto the three boys. I'm sure that's what sent him off."

"Did you see him, Kathy? His face?" Neil's eyes showed his alarm, though he spoke calmly.

"He wore a red and black chequered jacket and a ski cap. He had on goggles — I couldn't really see his face. He carried a rifle." Her voice trembled despite her efforts to avoid panic. "He wasn't after game, Neil. He followed us. I watched for him. I saw him moving right along with us!"

"It could be the same man who fired when Larry and you were on the pond. That bullet was meant for you, Kathy. Or for Larry." He shook his head in bewilderment. "It's insane."

"Twice here and once on the Taconic." She had to be objective. Her life or Larry's — or both their lives — depended on that. "It's a pattern."

"What happened on the Taconic?" Neil demanded.

Kathy filled him in, as briefly as possible, on what occurred the night of their trip to Salem.

"I thought he was a drunk," Kathy recalled. "And Christmas Day on the pond I thought some irresponsible hunter shot in our direction. But I can't believe those were accidents, Neil. Not now."

Neil was pale.

"Kathy, it isn't safe for you to be up here. I hate to think of your going back to New York ahead of schedule, but —"

"Neil, I was followed up here," she pinpointed. "From New York." She sighed in bewilderment. "Who would want to kill Larry or me? *Why?*"

"Let's go into town and discuss this with the police."

"What can the police do?" Kathy countered. "The force is too small to put a guard on the house. Besides, what do we have to offer the police?" She forced herself to be realistic. "A possible drunken driver, an overly zealous hunter — and my suspicions today that we were being stalked in the woods. Nobody will take this seriously."

"I do," Neil insisted. "Kathy, neither Larry nor you is to leave this house. Not until we know who's responsible. I'm going down to talk to the police — even though we have nothing substantial to offer them. I'll ask them to keep their eyes open for strangers around town." He smiled faintly. "In a town this size that isn't hard to do."

"Don't tell Mrs McArdle," Kathy cautioned.

"She'd be terribly upset."

"I'm upset," Neil admitted. "I won't relax until we know who's roaming around our woods with a rifle in hand."

Chapter Twenty-Eight

Randall pulled to a jolting stop before the motel unit. He charged out of the car and into his room. Rifle under one arm. What the hell crazy kind of luck was he running into, anyway? When they moved into that clearing, he could have nailed the kid if those creeps hadn't been there!

The other kid would have gone digging, and Larry would have been standing there. *Why did those three creepy jerks have to be there at the dump?*

He thrust the rifle onto the shelf again. He peeled off his jacket, pulled off his boots, and threw himself onto the bed. God, his feet were cold from standing in that rotten snow. And to miss the kid, when he was so close! His head was pounding wildly now. In a few minutes he'd get up and take a pill.

Right now all he wanted was to lie here in the warmth. To feel the ice leaving his feet. He wouldn't be going through this if it wasn't for Anita. She had a nerve leading him on the way she did. All those promises.

Only one other time had he let himself be tricked this way. But he was a kid then. Fifteen. He didn't know the score the way he did now.

He gazed up at the ceiling and visualised that girl. Betsy, he recalled. That was her name. She was little and pretty and adoring. Finally he took her to a drive-in movie. Mom always got sore when he took the car, but he was almost sixteen. Mom had taught him to drive when he was fourteen.

His face tightened as he remembered that night. It was cold at the movie, but he figured they wouldn't be cold for long. They sat there eating hamburgers and drinking root beer until the place went dark. Then he wanted to move into the back seat. Betsy refused. Hell, every girl in the school was ready to lie down for him. He could have had anybody he wanted.

"OK," he'd told her. "We're leaving." He wouldn't sit there and watch a movie with a foot of space between them.

He drove out of the drive-in and down the road.

"Where're you going?" She had been outraged when he turned off the road into a dark lane. Nobody would be there tonight. It was cold and a school night.

"Come on, baby," he'd coaxed again. "Why do you think I asked you to go to a drive-in movie?"

"You said you wanted to see the picture," she stammered. "That's what you said."

She fought him off when he tried to put his hand under her sweater. That made him see red. She had a nerve carrying on this way. She'd led him on.

After a while she stopped struggling. She didn't scream. She'd die of shame if anybody walked in on them. She lay there like a chunk of dead wood. Just yelling out once when he got there. It had been rotten for him.

He took her home, and she ran into the house like the devil was after her. Two hours later the police came to the house. He hadn't figured she'd have the nerve. His face tightened as he remembered the ugliness that followed.

Even now he could hear his mother screaming at him. Calling him every filthy name she could think of. But all the time her mind was working on a way to get him in the clear. She didn't want to soil the family name. That was all she cared about — she wasn't worried about his hide.

Mom went straight to her boss. That fancy attorney. The old boy knew who to go to for help. Mom raised the money. Money is power. Money got him off the hook.

His eyes gloated in recall. Remembering the showdown night when the attorney went to talk to Betsy's parents. He'd stood outside the window, pushing away the thorns on the rose bush as he stared through the sheer curtains. One window was open enough so he could hear what was being said inside.

"Mrs Townsend, you withdraw the charges, or we'll have to go into court with witnesses who'll swear they've had relations with your daughter before Randall. You don't want the whole town hearing things like that about Betsy, do you?"

"It's a lie!" Mrs Townsend shrieked. He'd thought she was going to have a heart attack. Betsy's father tried to calm her down. "It's a filthy, rotten lie!"

"Get out of here, Mr Kendrick!" Mr Townsend's voice had trembled with frustration. He knew the lawyer had them nailed. "Get out of here before I break your neck."

"I hope you rot in hell for your lousy lies!" Mrs Townsend's voice broke. "You'll get yours someday!"

But Mr Kendrick had gone on to become a county judge. He was one of the richest men in the state by now.

Randall stirred restlessly on the bed. Another day gone. He'd have to grab that kid fast. Somewhere in the next three days he was going to kill that kid. And if Kathy got in the way, she'd go with Larry.

They had no idea he was after them yesterday. It was those three dumb teenagers at the dump who screwed him. Tomorrow he'd be back at the old stand. Waiting to get Larry on target. Ready for that one minute he needed. The one right minute — and it was mission accomplished.

Chapter Twenty-Nine

Randall awoke the following morning with a devastating headache despite the long sleep. Another pill, he promised himself reluctantly. He hated taking the pills. They dulled his thinking.

He pulled himself up in bed, and the memory of yesterday smacked him in the face. Frustration beat a hammer against his head. So close, and to lose out.

OK. Get up. Dress. Go have breakfast and stake out the house again. Nobody would be watching for him. They didn't know he was there yesterday.

Kathy had been playing some silly game with the kids. *"Let's see how fast we can walk,"* he mimicked in his mind. She was cold. She wanted to get back indoors. Those creeps digging in the dump spoiled everything.

He showered — enjoying the hot spray across the back of his neck. He massaged the tenseness in his shoulder blades. He'd have to wait about thirty minutes before he went out in this weather after a shower. The oft-repeated exhortations of his mother during his growing-up years moved involuntarily into his thoughts.

"Randall, you don't go out after a shower for at least thirty minutes. Your pores are all open."

If he went down to Rio, he'd send the old lady

a card from there, he decided in a spurt of good humour. Just: *'Hi, having a great time.'* That would set her on her ear. Let her wonder what he was doing down in Rio.

Mom used to keep telling him how he was going to come to a terrible end if he didn't change his ways. What did she get out of life? Still a legal secretary. Pinching pennies. At least, she was still at it when he cut out of UCLA, with the cheque she'd sent him to see him through the next quarter of school.

He dawdled over dressing, mentally reproaching himself for missing out thus far. But today would be different. He brought down the gun, handled it with pride. Today he was going to do it. He had this weird feeling inside that told him this was the day.

He flipped open the Venetian blind and stared outdoors. There had been a heavy snowfall during the night. At least two inches, he judged from the pile-up on the cars. Probably more. Nobody could complain they weren't getting enough snow this holiday season.

Today he would be prepared for the weather. Double socks inside his boots. A thermal undershirt beneath his flannel shirt. He wouldn't mind the cold. Today it was going to happen.

He brought down the chequered jacket, hesitated, discarded it for the shearling. The shearling was more inconspicuous up there in the woods. Take along a scarf to keep his neck warm.

He reached into a drawer for one of the Hermes

scarves Anita had bought for him from one of her frequent sorties into Bergdorf's, folded it about his neck with a complacent inspection of himself in the mirror. Would anybody around here believe what Anita had spent on the scarf?

He left the motel and settled himself behind the wheel of the car. He'd have to drive slowly. Road conditions were lousy. He stopped off at the Log Cabin for breakfast, then headed for Salem.

He made the left at the traffic light, drove out of the village limits. He went past the house and turned off onto a side road, parked beside a snow-covered field. Not a soul in sight this morning. Everything working for him today.

He entered the school property and climbed high above the house. The air was fragrant with the scent of wood burning somewhere inside the house. Smoke billowed from the chimney.

This morning four children were taking turns being pulled around the pond in a sledge, in pairs, by a man in a snowmobile. That must be the guy Kathy called Neil. He was in charge for the holidays. *Where the hell was Larry?*

Restless and cold, Randall paced about in the woods, high above the pond. Then he moved to the area of the falling-in barn. He squinted at the sky with distaste. Not one damn bit of sun to cut the cold.

He remained cautiously behind the barn. Positioning himself where he had a clear view of the area behind the house yet avoiding the pen. It

176

didn't take much to set off the geese.

Kathy would come out with Larry when the others went inside, he told himself. Larry got self-conscious with the other kids, most likely. Kathy would drive the snowmobile around the pond and tow Larry on the sledge. No sweat to pick him off with the rifle. One, two, three — and it would be over. Anita's belated Christmas present.

The rifle under one arm, Randall walked steadily up and down a thirty foot strip behind the barn. Keeping his eyes on the house. Listening to the laughter of the children on the sledge. Christ, how long before they went inside? Before Kathy came out with Larry?

He pulled the scarf higher about his throat. Drew the wool knit cap over his ears. No goggles this morning, he had decided. He needed perfect vision. No mistakes. Time was too tight.

He stiffened to attention. With much high-spirited horseplay the kids were charging down the incline from the pond. The guy was taking the snowmobile down a path towards the road. He waited until the kids were inside the house before he cut across the road onto the field on the other side and circled exuberantly for a few minutes.

Now the geese began to squawk, but in a moment they quieted down. Wary of the geese Randall inched down the far side of the barn. He watched while the guy — Neil — returned to the house. Randall looked at his watch. They must be having lunch now. After lunch Kathy would come out with Larry.

He fished in his jacket pocket for the crushed, near-full package of cigarettes. At a time like this he smoked. He'd have to be careful around the dry timber of the old barn. All he had to do was to start a fire.

He chain-smoked for an hour. *He wouldn't leave until he had accomplished what he had come here to do.* Then he spied two children emerging from the rear door of the house. Larry and the little girl who had been with him in the woods. Hand in hand they moved towards the pen. Right away the geese began to honk.

"Quiet, King! Quiet, Sandy!" Larry giggled as he skipped along with the little girl. "We're just coming to visit you."

"We're not supposed to be out here without Neil," the little girl reminded. Her voice carrying to Randall. *Why weren't they supposed to be out here?* Unease infiltrated Randall.

"We're together," Larry said. "You'd see that fox if it came out of the woods."

The children had been told that a fox was running around in the woods, Randall interpreted. *They knew he was prowling around here. He had to do it now.*

"Ellie, go in the house and get some corn for the geese," Larry wheedled. "I think they're hungry."

"I shouldn't leave you by yourself," Ellie worried.

"I'll stay right here with the geese." Larry was

calm. "If the fox comes down this way, they'll make a lot of noise. Go on, Ellie. You can do it faster by yourself."

Randall watched while Ellie scurried to the house. He waited until she disappeared inside. Now. That minute he needed. But not the rifle, his mind warned. The shot would bring them all running. He'd be too close for comfort.

He pulled the scarf from around his neck. Rolled it into a slender, silken, lethal rope. Now he inched forward, keeping behind the barn so he couldn't be seen.

The geese began to honk loudly when he emerged from behind the barn into view. Let them. Larry thought they were just complaining about being kept in the pen. Larry wasn't really worried about a fox coming down from the woods. He looked serene and undisturbed.

He moved forward noiselessly. Larry was just a few feet away now. *Easy, Randall. Easy.*

Chapter Thirty

"Ellie!" Walking into the kitchen Kathy stared in alarm. "Where's Larry?"

"Out by the pen. I came in to get corn —"

Oh God, Larry was out there alone! Kathy raced towards the back door without bothering to go for a coat.

"Kathy, he's all right. He's not scared," Ellie called after her as she pushed through the door.

She hurried towards the pen. From this angle Larry was obscured from view.

"Larry?" Her voice betrayed her anxiety.

"I'm right here, Kathy," Larry soothed. Guilty at being caught outdoors alone.

"Larry," she scolded as she approached him. "You know you're not supposed to be outside without Neil or me."

"Kathy!" Neil's voice cut through the crisp cold air.

"It's all right, Neil," she called back and then froze as her eyes focused on the colourful length of rolled-over silk that lay at Larry's feet.

"You'll catch cold running out in this weather without a coat," Neil rebuked, stripping off his jacket. "Here, put this on."

"Neil . . ." she said softly and pointed to the scarf that lay in the snow.

"Someone was here. Take Larry and go back into the house."

As she reached for Larry's hand, she heard a twig snap no more than twenty feet from them. *Behind the barn.*

"Neil, he's still here!"

Gesturing for silence Neil sprinted past the pen and disappeared behind the barn. Within moments she heard a grunt of pain, the sound — again — of twigs broken underfoot.

"Neil?" Her heart pounded in terror. "Larry, stay right here." While she moved towards the barn, she saw Ellie coming out of the back door of the house. "Ellie, come stay with Larry."

She circled around to the far side of the far side of the barn and stopped dead. Neil lay at their feet. Blood oozed from a wound in his scalp. She dropped to her haunches.

"Neil?" She inspected him anxiously. He was stirring now. His words incoherent.

"I'm all right," he managed to tell her. "Somebody was hiding behind a tree. He clipped me over the head." With Kathy's help he struggled to his feet. "Kathy, he was after Larry." Their eyes met in comprehension.

"Can you make it to the house?" She inspected Neil's scalp with solicitude. "That wound has to be cleaned up."

"I'm groggy, but I can make it." He managed a wry smile. "Let's go."

"Neil, what happened?" Ellie clung to Larry's hand.

181

"Somebody clobbered me." He was being matter-of-fact so as not to escalate the children's alarm. "But I've got a hard head. I'll be all right."

"Why did they do that?" Larry was suddenly fearful in his dark little world.

"We don't know yet, darling," Kathy told him. Striving for calm. "But the police will find out."

Mrs McArdle was sitting at the table in the kitchen over coffee when they walked into the room. She looked up in shock, immediately conscious that something was very wrong. In a few words Neil explained what had happened.

Mrs McArdle rose from her chair.

"Let's get that cut fixed up. Then you'd better call the police."

"Neil, I think you're going to need a couple of stitches." Kathy hovered over the wound in his scalp, then turned to Mrs McArdle. "Where's the nearest hospital?"

"Cambridge," Mrs McArdle said. "You better drive right over there."

Kathy was relieved that the van sat in the driveway. No time would be wasted bringing it out. Neil and she climbed into the front seat. She insisted on driving. The children watched their departure. The holiday spirit had evaporated.

"Drive into town and south on 22," Neil directed. "Just keep rolling till we reach the hospital. We take a right at the light, onto 372."

They were silent for a few moments. Neil gingerly held the pads of sterile gauze Mrs McArdle had provided to the scalp wound.

"Neil, who would want to kill Larry?" Kathy asked sombrely. To follow them all the way from New York to Salem with murderous intent. "I'm not imagining that someone meant to strangle Larry."

"He meant to." Neil's face was taut with anger. "You scared him away when you ran out of the house. He dropped the scarf and ran. He panicked when he realised I was after him. He hid behind that spruce tree and hit me when I charged past. I ran right into the trap," he said ruefully.

"Why would anybody want to murder Larry? It's senseless."

"I could understand a kidnapping," Neil said. "I gather the family is wealthy. But murder?"

"It has to be someone sick." Kathy shuddered. "Terribly sick."

"We'll stop by the State Police on the way back," Neil decided. "I don't know what they can do, but we have to report this. They're just ahead there, past that attractive country store."

"I must phone New York," Kathy said after a moment. "Mrs Cantrell's housekeeper will know where to contact her."

"Stop looking so upset." Neil reached to touch her hand on the wheel. "I know this seems like a nightmare, but we won't let anything happen to Larry."

Deliberately Neil began to talk about activities at the school, pausing now and then to point out local landmarks.

"We must go to King's for coffee and cake

183

someday," he said as Kathy turned off Route 22 onto 372. "It's probably the greatest bakery in the country. Of course," he chuckled, "we can't tell Mrs McArdle when we go. She'd be hurt."

At the hospital Kathy turned as Neil directed. For an instant her eyes lingered on the white gauze he held to his scalp. It was stained, but he wasn't losing a lot of blood, she decided in relief. But stitches were needed to bring the wound together.

"I know this is a ghastly time to talk about us," Neil began sombrely, "but I have to say it again. I'm in love with you. I don't need a month or six months to know it. I knew it from the first evening when we sat in front of the Franklin stove and talked till three. I won't try to rush you into marriage, but I'd like you to know that's my goal." He grinned. "I'm conventional about some things."

"It's happening so fast I'm scared," Kathy admitted. "Like you said, let's don't rush it. OK?"

"OK."

Kathy pulled up before the vast grounds of the hospital. A collection of buildings, largely modern, with much expanse of glass. An astonishingly impressive hospital for so small a town. Kathy drove around the battery of cars in search of a space to park.

"There to the left." Neil spotted a driver pulling out. "They do a thriving business here."

Kathy parked. Neil and she followed the signs that led to the Emergency entrance. Almost immediately a doctor and nurse were examining his injury. The doctor inquired if Neil had been unconscious.

"Only for a moment," Neil told him.

"Then we don't need to bring in a neurologist," the doctor said leisurely.

"You have one on staff?" Neil asked interestedly.

The doctor grinned. "We have one on call. He lives down in Schenectady. We call. He hops on a plane, lands at the airport here in Cambridge. He's here in ten minutes. All right, we'll go inside and do some hemstitching on your scalp."

Kathy sat on a bench in the Emergency reception room. Four times Larry's life had been on the line. Why hadn't they realised this right from the beginning? On impulse Kathy rose to her feet and approached the desk. She asked if she might make a phone call.

She dialled the house and waited impatiently for Mrs McArdle to answer.

"Neil's fine," she reported. "He just needs two or three stitches. But please don't let Larry out of the house. Don't let him out of your sight."

By the time Kathy and Neil left the hospital, fresh snow had begun to fall. The snow beneath was turning to ice. Kathy drove with cautious slowness.

They pulled off the road before the State Police headquarters, left the car to walk inside. Kathy stood by quietly while Neil reported what had transpired.

"Did anybody get a look at this man?" the policeman probed. "Did he leave anything behind?"

"None of us saw him," Neil said. "I was running after him when I got this." His hand touched his scalp. "He left a scarf behind," Neil remembered. "I don't know if it'll be of any help."

"I'll follow you back to the house," the policeman told them. "Let's see what we can pick up."

At the house the children were eager to listen in on the conversation between the policeman and Neil and Kathy. Mrs McArdle shifted them into the living room, bribed them with cookies and apple juice to remain out of hearing.

"Murder is always a nasty business, but it turns me sick when somebody goes after a kid." The policeman shook his head in distaste. "We'll see what we can do with the scarf —"

"It's quite expensive," Kathy pointed out. "See the label?"

"We'll run it down," the policeman promised and rose to his feet. "Meanwhile, I suggest you notify the little boy's parents. Maybe they can come up with answers. We'd like to talk to them."

Kathy went to the telephone and dialled New York. Martha should be back at the apartment by now. She answered on the second ring, and was startled to be hearing from Kathy.

"May I have Mrs Cantrell's phone number down in Palm Beach?" Kathy tried to sound casual.

"Has something happened to Larry?" Instantly Martha was upset.

"Larry's fine," Kathy reassured her. "But I must talk to Mrs Cantrell."

"I'm sorry," Martha apologised. "Nobody can reach her. She called last night to say that she was going out on some friend's yacht. She said she couldn't be reached till New Year's Eve, when she'll be back in Palm Beach for some party."

"Martha, are you sure?" Kathy pressed. "This is urgent."

"She gave me no number," Martha reiterated. Disapproval crept into her voice. "I guess she didn't want to be bothered when she was on a holiday."

"Thank you, Martha." *How could Larry's mother go away without leaving a number where she could be reached?*

"You're sure Larry's all right?" Martha asked. Still anxious.

"Larry's fine," Kathy insisted. "Wait, I'll let you talk to him." Only then would Martha truly believe her.

The responsibility for keeping Larry alive was theirs. But they didn't know who was after him. Or why. *How did they protect him?*

Chapter Thirty-One

Randall slumped over a ham and cheese sandwich at Stewart's. A 'do-it-yourself' sundae tray at his elbow. His eyes smouldered in frustration. What kind of crazy luck was dodging his footsteps? He was ready to drop the scarf about the kid's neck — Larry didn't even know he was there — when Kathy yelled out the door that way.

He left the scarf behind, but nobody would make anything of it. Bergdorf's sold hundreds of them. Did they know why he clobbered the creep? They knew he was up to no good — but they didn't know *what* he was up to there at the pen. Nobody would figure out he meant to kill the kid.

Tonight. Finish it off tonight. He'd had it with these crazy mistakes. Anita was down in Palm Beach roasting herself in the sun in one of those fancy bikinis she took down there with her. For her age she looked sensational in a bikini. For her age. Damn Anita! Living it up down there while he cooled his heels in a broken-down motel room.

He gestured the waitress to bring on the ice-cream. When it arrived, he dumped lavish scoops of chocolate syrup, marshmallow whip, and nuts on top. He ate with an air of vindictive pleasure. For a few minutes he forgot the grinding ache in his head.

The trouble was, he'd been too cautious all

along. So scared to stick out his neck. He had to do it today. He wanted out of this town. He could see himself, standing in the cemetery before the open grave while Anita cried her head off. Anita would feel so rotten. Worse than she had ever felt in her life. He owed her that.

He'd drive out to the house again. Nobody saw him — he'd cut out as soon as Kathy came out the door. She couldn't have seen him. Not the way he lit out. That guy couldn't have seen him. He got the jerk from the back.

Wait until dark. Go out with the gun stuck in his waist. Creep around to the far side of the house — away from the pen. The geese wouldn't know he was there on that side of the house. Not if he was careful. Shoot the kid through the window, and run.

I don't have to worry about what'll happen after I shoot the kid. There'll be an uproar inside the house. While they're carrying on, I'll run. Keep the car a hundred feet down the road. Hurry back behind the wheel and get out fast.

I can do it.

Chapter Thirty-Two

The paper bag from the Chinese 'take-away' tucked in one arm, David Ames unlocked the door to his apartment, walked inside with an air of dejection. Manhattan could be such a damnably lonely place at this time of year, he thought grimly as he walked into the kitchen. *Where the hell was Larry?*

He'd called the apartment, the house at East Hampton, even Larry's paediatrician. There'd been no response at his ex-mother-in-law's townhouse. He was consumed by guilt. He and Larry were supposed to spend the holidays together.

He brought down a plate, collected a tray, walked back into the living room to flip on the TV. Programming during the holidays tended to be repeats, he thought in distaste — but the sound of voices was oddly comforting. He transferred dumplings, fried rice, and sesame chicken on to a plate — ate without tasting. Damn, there ought to be somebody in this town who could tell him where he could find Larry!

Again, he went over in his mind his contacts with Anita's circle. There was nobody to call — and ten to one her friends were holed up in some exotic spot for the holidays. Where did Martha go on her time off? She had family somewhere in Queens, he recalled. What was her last name? He searched his mind. Brown, he remembered in total rejection. It would be New Year's Eve before he could call every Brown in the Queen's telephone directory.

Should he try the apartment on the chance that Martha was back now? Not likely, he derided. But give it a whirl. He put aside his plate and reached for the phone. He dialled and waited while the phone rang in Anita's apartment. He hadn't really expected anybody to be there, he taunted himself and took the receiver from his ear.

"Hello . . . Hello?" Unmistakably Martha's voice, faintly breathless, as though she'd just come into the apartment and had rushed to pick up the phone.

"Merry Christmas, Martha," he said jubilantly. "This is David Ames. I've been trying for days to get through to Larry. Could you tell me where he is?"

"He's upstate, Mr Ames." David heard the reproach in her voice. "Mrs Cantrell hired some young woman to take him to a school up there for the holidays."

"Where, Martha?" David demanded. "Where is he?"

"I think I might have the address around here somewhere. If you hold on, I'll try to find it . . ."

Despite the efforts of Neil and herself to lighten the atmosphere in the house, Kathy was conscious of the almost unbearable tension at the dinner table. The small white patch atop Neil's head was mute evidence of violence. The children were not sure how Larry was involved. They sensed he was — and they were scared.

Larry sneezed. Kathy turned anxiously to him. That was the fourth time. He was coming down with a cold.

"How would you all like to go on a moonlight sleigh ride right to the top of the mountain some night?" Neil asked in a burst of inspiration.

"Tonight!" Jamie demanded, his face glowing. "Let's do it tonight."

"Yeah, yeah," Livvy picked up. "Let's go tonight."

"There's lots of snow on the ground," Jean persuaded. "And the moon is out."

"I don't know if I can arrange it that fast," Neil hedged, then softened at the look of disappointment that he saw on the children's faces. "Let me phone the man with the sleigh and see what we can work out," he capitulated and rose to his feet.

"I'll go with you," Kathy said quickly. "Call on the living room extension," she said pointedly.

"Sure," Neil agreed.

Kathy and Neil walked into the living room. Neil closed the door behind them. Ostensibly to eliminate the dining room sounds.

"Neil, I don't dare let Larry leave the house tonight," Kathy told him.

"He'll be safe surrounded by all of us," Neil tried to placate. "Nobody can get to him."

"I don't dare take him out of the house after

what happened today," Kathy reiterated. Must they sit here in the house until it was time to go back to New York? Could they reach New York safely? "I'm responsible for Larry's staying alive and well."

"Tomorrow I'll hire three security guards," Neil said after deliberation. "To work in eight hour shifts around the clock. One of them will go into New York with you when you leave with Larry. They'll be billed to Mrs Cantrell by the school, but I'm sure she won't object to that. Larry doesn't know someone's after him —"

"He's suspicious," Kathy said worriedly. "All the children are."

"They don't know," Neil soothed. "I'll tell everybody the security guards are here to catch the poacher. A crazy hunter who ignores 'No Hunting' signs. That'll make you feel more comfortable, won't it?"

"Yes." She managed a grateful smile. Thank God for Neil.

"I'll have to tell the kids we're postponing the sleigh ride," he said briskly. "We'll do it another time."

"No, don't disappoint them," Kathy urged. "I'll keep Larry in the house. I suspect he's coming down with a cold. That's a logical excuse."

"I don't like to leave you in the house when I'm away." His eyes were troubled. "Just Larry, Mrs McArdle, and you. No, we'll postpone the sleigh ride."

"Neil, please don't. The children have little

enough of a Christmas. We'll stay in the house with all the lights on and the drapes drawn tight. Nobody coming by will realise there are just the three of us here. Let the geese out of the pen. At night they'll stay close to the house. If anybody tried to approach, they'll run him off with their honking. Besides, he wouldn't dare try anything after this afternoon." She prayed that he wouldn't. Now they knew there was a definite *somebody*. The patch atop Neil's head attested to that. "Please, Neil. Don't deprive the children of the sleigh ride."

"All right." But Neil was uneasy. "Be sure all the doors are locked. All the drapes drawn tight. Keep a fire going in both the fireplace and the Franklin stove. Leave lights on in several rooms. It'll seem that people are in the house. A lot of people," he emphasised. "And I'll let the geese out front when we leave." He reached for the phone. "I'll call about the sleigh."

When the arrangements were made, Neil sent the children up to their rooms for proper clothing. Larry was disappointed that he was to stay home. He sat silent, his face desolate. Kathy searched her mind for some treat that would make this deprivation less painful.

"I'm going into town to a party," Mrs McArdle said without realising the effect this announcement would have on Kathy and Neil. "I'll be back by midnight. If it's all right, I'll leave as soon as I stack the dishes in the dishwasher."

Kathy saw Neil tense in alarm. Kathy imperceptibly shook her head to forestall his making a change in plans.

"No problem. I'll stack the dishes, Mrs McArdle," Kathy offered. "Go on to your party right now. And have fun."

"The farmer with the sleigh is picking us up in half an hour," Neil said sombrely when Mrs McArdle had taken off. He was still troubled by this switch in plan.

"Kathy, can't I go, too?" Larry wheedled now. "I've stopped sneezing."

"Darling, we don't want to take any chances on your coming down with a bad cold," Kathy rejected gently and saw Larry's hopeful smile evaporate. Poor baby. "You know what you and I will do?" she plotted convivially. "You and I will make a layer cake." Cake mixes were kept on a shelf, to be utilised as a bad weather diversion for the children. "You'll beat the batter, but you'll have to beat it a lot so it'll be light and fluffy. All right?"

Larry considered this for an instant. "I'd rather go on the sleigh ride," he admitted wistfully. "But I'll help you make the cake."

Chapter Thirty-Three

Randall flipped open the venetian blind and gazed outdoors. It was dark enough now. The moon had slid behind a cluster of clouds. The stars were nowhere in evidence.

All right, he ordered himself. Get into the car and drive over to the school. No, stop first for something to eat. That might help his headache. He hadn't eaten since breakfast.

He would park about a hundred feet past the house. There would be no traffic to speak of on the road tonight. The few passing traffic wouldn't notice the beat-up black car sitting at the side of the road.

He pulled on his shearling jacket, that would blend with the scenery, and reached into the top dresser drawer to bring out his hand gun. He stared at the gun for a moment, as though willing it to be used tonight, then slid it into a comfortable position at his waist.

With the car keys in one hand he reached with the other for the gloves that lay across the bed. Take a scarf along. He liked the feel of silk around his neck. Pity he lost the fancy one yesterday.

A faint smile about his mouth he walked from the motel unit to his car. It would all be over in a little while. Just the way he had planned.

He should have done it this way the first night up here.

He swore at his car's usual reluctance to move into action in cold weather. Finally the car rolled out of the parking area onto the road. He would do the job, and then he would go over to the bar and chat with Chris.

If anything happens, Chris will swear I was at the bar with her all evening. But nothing will go wrong. In the morning I'll check out of the motel and drive back to New York.

It won't take long for Anita to hear the bad news. She'll be on the first plane out of Palm Beach. She'll be so sick she'll want to die. It's just what she deserves.

Chapter Thirty-Four

Kathy finished stacking the dishes in the dishwasher. Neil moved methodically about the house, drawing all the drapes snug against the night.

"I feel uneasy leaving Larry and you alone in the house," Neil said seriously when he returned to the kitchen.

"Nothing can happen to us here," Kathy insisted with a fragile hold on conviction. "The house will be locked tight. Nobody'll know the two of us are the only ones here."

Outside the geese set up a clamour sure to discourage any intruder. The neighbour with the sleigh was arriving. He was circling around to the rear. Neil crossed to the switch to flip on the battery of outdoor spotlights that bathed the area surrounding the house in daylight brightness.

"Kids!" Kathy called out. "The sleigh's here."

The youngsters surged into the kitchen.

"Are we really going to the top of the mountain?" Ellie asked avidly.

"All the way to the top," Kathy said, and belatedly tried to temper her enthusiasm. Larry was still wistful about not accompanying them. "And while you're up there, Larry and I will be making the most luscious cherry layer cake."

"All right, everybody," Neil ordered in high

spirits. "Out the back and into the sleigh. The horses are impatient." He turned to Kathy. His eyes still anxious. "Make sure you lock all the doors. I'm sorry I suggested this safari."

"It'll be fun for the children." Kathy could hear their laughter as they moved out into the night. "And stop worrying about Larry and me," she whispered. "We'll be fine."

"Be careful," he reiterated and pulled her close for a moment. "If you hear anything disturbing, call the police. Don't hesitate to call them, Kathy."

"I won't," she promised. Enjoying his solicitude.

She closed the door and locked it. Knowing Neil was waiting on the other side to hear the click of the lock. He himself had locked the other doors. Now she went into the living room, where Larry sat in a rocker before the fire.

"Larry, we can't sit around doing nothing," she teased and reached out a hand to him. "Let's get going with that cake."

A healthy fire crackled in the Franklin stove as they went through the steps of preparing the layer cake for the oven. Kathy flipped on the kitchen radio to bring in a flow of recorded music. Nevertheless, she was starkly conscious of their aloneness in the huge old house. Every small outdoor sound registered in her mind.

By the time they had the cake in the oven, Larry was yawning. Anxiously Kathy felt his forehead. No temperature, she decided in relief. Just a slight cold. This sleepiness was part of it.

"Tell you what, Larry," she proposed brightly. "You go upstairs into your bedroom and take a nap. I'll call you when it's time to take the cake out of the oven."

"What about the icing?" Larry suppressed another yawn.

"We won't make it until we bring the cake out. And the cake has to cool before we ice it, remember."

"All right," Larry accepted philosophically and held up a hand for Kathy to take. "But call me before you take the cake out of the oven. I want to be there. Then I'll help you with the icing."

Chapter Thirty-Five

Randall pulled up before the Log Cabin. They'd be closing soon, but he didn't mean to waste much time over dinner. He'd eat and get out. He left the car, pausing to inspect the horse-drawn sleigh that waited off to one side for its passengers. A man chewing on a pipe carried on a one-sided conversation with the two horses.

Randall walked to the entrance at the side of the structure and waited to allow an exodus of children with an adult. He felt a trickle of excitement. The children from the school! With that guy Neil, whom he clobbered on the head behind the barn this afternoon.

"How was that hot chocolate?" Neil asked. "Warm you all up?"

"Sure," a red-haired boy said exuberantly. "Good as Mrs McArdle's."

"Where did Mrs McArdle go tonight?" one of the little girls asked curiously.

"To a party in town. She'll be back late," Neil reported. "Now let's go keep our date with that mountain."

Larry wasn't with them. Kathy and he were at the house. *Alone.* The housekeeper wouldn't be back until late. The others were going on a sleigh ride up the mountain. Terrific!

With soaring confidence Randall went into the

Log Cabin and sat at a table by the window. He ordered a roast beef sandwich and coffee, knowing he could be out of the restaurant in ten minutes.

Through the window he watched the sleigh head south. They'd be gone at least an hour. Probably longer. No sweat. He'd accomplish the mission and be back at the bar with Chris before the others returned to the house.

Driving away from the Log Cabin, inching along because of the ice beneath the snow, he switched on the radio. A newscaster was reporting on a murder in the Glens Falls area.

"The young woman, twenty-one, was viciously hacked to death. The house had been ransacked, pointing to a motive of robbery. So far the police have no clues . . ."

Randall's mind was active. He didn't even have to worry about somebody hearing the gun shot. There was nobody at the house except Larry and Kathy. The nearest house on either side was out of hearing range. Only open fields across the road.

He was devising a whole new routine. He'd park right around the bend in the road. He'd go up to the house and tell Kathy the battery in his car had conked out. She'd let him inside to phone the garage. Or maybe he'd ask her if he could borrow jump leads and her car. He'd get into the house.

He'd keep on his gloves. That way there'd be no fingerprints. This time he'd leave nothing behind — except two bodies. Mess up the house so it would look like robbery. The cops would blame it on the guy who killed the girl in Glens Falls. How far was Glens Falls from here? Thirty, thirty-five miles? Pity Kathy had to get it, too.

He was whistling along with the radio as he turned off at the traffic light in Salem. Switch off the radio, he told himself. Keep his mind clear. Keep his gloves on. Don't take a chance of leaving prints behind.

Who said there was no such thing as a perfect crime? Hundreds of guys walked the streets — beating a murder rap. He was about to add to that number.

He approached the house slowly. A lot of rooms were lighted. That was because Kathy was uptight. She didn't want anybody to know she was alone with the kid. Had she heard the news on the radio about that murder up in Glens Falls? That wouldn't exactly calm her.

Drive past the house. Make it look like the battery conked out a hundred feet past the driveway. It was a snap, he told himself on a tide of optimism. Kathy would let him in the house, and he'd do his job. No fuss. Nothing. The cops would look for the guy who murdered that chick up in Glens Falls.

He pulled to a stop close to the edge of the road. He left the car without bothering to lock it. He trudged through the snow and started up the driveway. Damn those geese! Right away they had to honk! But tonight it didn't matter.

Suddenly floodlights bathed the outdoor area.

Kathy had heard the geese. She was nervous. Or maybe she just figured some animal was after the geese.

He cut off from the driveway and walked across to the front steps. He went up the steps and knocked at the door.

"Who is it?" Kathy's voice. She was scared.

"Rick," he said briskly. "I was driving up the road and my battery went dead . . ."

The door swung wide. Kathy smiled at him in relief.

"Rick! Come in!"

Chapter Thirty-Six

Kathy closed the door quickly behind Rick, against the sharp night cold. When she heard his knock, she had been frightened for a moment. Her first instinct had been to run to the phone and call for help. And here it was Rick, she thought thankfully, stranded down the road.

"I don't know why the car conked out on me," Randall said with disgust. "I had it completely overhauled before I came up. I was on my way to West Hebron for a poker game with this guy I met on the slopes. I figure it's the battery. It acted up a couple of days ago. Do you have any jump leads?"

"No, I don't," she said apologetically. Robin always told her to keep jump leads in the boot of the car. "Neil probably has some in the van. He's out with the kids. He took them on a sleigh ride. They ought to be back soon." She hesitated. No, she couldn't tell him to go look in the van. Besides, the car was probably locked. "Come out to the kitchen and have some coffee with me."

What a relief to find Rick on the doorstep this way! Alone in the kitchen her imagination had been running amok. Every night sound outside unnerved her. Belatedly she remembered that she had not locked the front door. But that didn't matter. Rick was here.

He sniffed appreciatively. "What's in the oven?"

"A layer cake." She moved rapidly towards the kitchen. "It'll be ready to take out in a few minutes."

In the kitchen she checked the cake. It needed to stay in another few minutes, as she'd surmised. The timer still had four minutes to go.

"Did you hear the late news?" He stood before the Franklin stove. Still bundled up in his shearling jacket and gloves. "Terrible murder over near Glens Falls. The girl was hacked to death. They just found her body."

Kathy felt herself pale. "How awful!" She recoiled from such horror. Especially today she reacted strongly to violence. "Where is Glens Falls?" She had some vague notion of its being in the same county.

"Not far. Maybe thirty miles from here," he guessed.

"Do the police know the motive?" The man this afternoon. The one who meant to strangle Larry. Was it that man?

"The police suspect robbery." He unbuttoned the top of his jacket. "The place was in a shambles."

"But to hack her up!" That was what Rick said — that she had been hacked to death. "That's a sick mind."

He smiled faintly. "Maybe he was a frustrated butcher."

Kathy gaped at him in shock. That was sick humour. "I'm sorry the cake isn't ready." She wished he had not made that awful joke about the murder. "Why don't you take off your jacket? It's so warm in here." Why was he looking at her so strangely? "Would you like to call the garage? Maybe somebody could come right out with a jump leads. I mean, if your friend is expecting you . . ." All at once she was uncomfortable with Rick.

"No, I'll wait for your friend to come back. Maybe he has jump leads."

"The coffee should be ready in a minute. It's probably hot enough now." She was talking compulsively. "I just had a cup a few minutes ago." She moved to the range. "Yes, it's perking again. I'll turn it off." Something was wrong here. What was it?

"Where's Larry?"

"Larry?" she stalled. *Why did he ask about Larry?* Her mind jumped to a fearful possibility. Rick was after Larry? He was on the Taconic that night . . .

"Larry," he repeated furiously. "Where's the kid?"

His eyes held hers. A cold wave of horror shot through her. Her eyes darted to the phone, and his gaze followed hers. He stalked across the room, ripped the phone cord from the wall.

"Larry's not here," she lied. "I told you. Neil took the children out for a sleigh ride up the mountain. Larry's with them."

"You're lying!" he shouted. "I saw them at the Log Cabin. Larry wasn't with them. He's here. Now you tell me where!"

"No!" Kathy shot back defiantly. "What do you want with him?"

"I have business with Larry," he said with menacing softness. "A little Christmas present for his bitch of a mother. You go get that kid and bring him here. And do it now."

"No!" Kathy's eyes blazed. Why didn't Neil come home? Rick would kill Larry. How could she stop him?

"I want that kid." He moved towards her and grabbed at her arm. "Tell me where he is."

"No," she reiterated. Rick was a psychotic killer! "No! I told you — he's not here." *Larry, hear me. Wake up and hide. Hide, Larry.*

"You're lying." He twisted her arm till she cried out. "Go get him."

"I won't let you hurt him!"

His hand shot out. It caught her on the side of her head. She felt herself falling. Her head hit a cabinet. She was losing consciousness. Oh, no, no. Oh, God, he'll kill Larry . . .

Chapter Thirty-Seven

Randall hung over Kathy's prostrate form. Damn her! Why didn't she tell him where the kid was? But Larry was somewhere in this house. He'd find him. Find him quick, before the others came back. Finish off Larry. Then come back for Kathy.

He left Kathy and stalked into the living room. Nobody here. Upstairs, he guessed. Larry would be in one of the bedrooms. He couldn't wander around alone. Maybe he was asleep already.

Randall raced up the stairs. Several of the bedrooms were lighted. He checked one after another, finding no one. Then he saw a door at the end of the hall. Larry had to be in there.

He opened the door into a tiny sitting room. Damn it, Larry wasn't here! And then he realised there was a room beyond. He pulled open the door at the other side of the room. Here he was greeted by darkness except for a night light in a wall plug.

Larry lay asleep on a bed. A stuffed dog clutched in his arms. Randall moved to the side of the bed. He was remembering his younger sister, years ago. She had hair like Larry's. He reached out with one gloved hand and pulled viciously at the silken hair, the way he used to pull his sister's.

Larry woke up. He cried out in terror. Randall tugged harder at the hair within his grasp. Larry screamed. His sister had screamed, too. Every time. He hated her yelling. It made his head ache.

"Shut up!" he ordered. "Shut up, Larry!"

"Randall?" Larry was startled. "What are you doing here?" He clung to the stuffed dog. His eyes wide. Seeing nothing.

"Be quiet, Larry. You just sit up, nice and easy. Do like I say, and I won't hurt you. Just sit up." He reached around his neck for the scarf and pulled it off. Now he rolled it up, prepared to drop it behind Larry's head. He didn't even need a gun. Just one minute more and it'd be all over.

"Drop that!"

Randall spun around in rage. White-faced but determined, Kathy hovered in the doorway. A hunting rifle in her hand. Aimed at him. Cool it, Randall. Cool it. You can handle this chick.

"Put down that rifle," he said with deceptive amusement.

"No." She moved forward slightly. "And keep your hands high," she ordered as he made a tentative move towards his waist with his right hand.

"You haven't the guts to shoot me," he taunted. "Put it down." He made a wary move towards her.

"Rick, don't make me shoot. I will," she warned. "For Larry I will."

"I'll bet it isn't even loaded." They wouldn't keep a loaded rifle in the house with children

210

around. Kathy wouldn't know how to load a rifle.

"I loaded it."

She was lying. He lunged forward. Grappled with her for the rifle. He could shoot her right now, but he didn't want the sounds of shots in the house until he was ready to take off. Nothing that would attract somebody passing by, he told himself with his more familiar caution.

"Let her go!" A strange masculine voice cut through the air. "Let her go!"

A man stood in the doorway. Tall, mid-thirties. Dangerously calm. Randall thrust Kathy, still clinging to the rifle, to one side and reached into his jacket for the gun at his waist. The stranger leapt towards him before he could shoot. The gun went sprawling across the room.

"Get Larry out of here!" the man shouted as he tangled with Randall. "Get him out of here!"

Who the hell was this creep? Where did he come from? He had to get his gun! Damn, he had to get his gun! There it was, right across the floor.

"Daddy!" Larry cried out in recognition. "Daddy, Daddy!"

Distracted by Larry's outcry, his father relaxed his hold. *Now. Get the gun.* Randall broke free and darted towards the gun. His hand was inches away from it, he howled with pain. Kathy had brought the rifle down against his spine.

Larry's father crossed to where the gun lay and bent to pick it up while Randall struggled to his feet.

"Daddy! Daddy! I can see! I can see!"

"Larry! Larry, baby!"

Run! Run now, while the guy was distracted. In a frenzy Randall bolted from the room and down the hall. Taking the stairs two at a time. He ignored the orders to stop. Get the hell out of here! The car was right down the road.

He raced out of the house and down the driveway. The geese honking. Bullets flew over his head, along with exhortations for him to stop. He didn't see the gritter swinging around the bend in the road.

Oh, God! God, no! Not again! No!

Chapter Thirty-Eight

"Stay in the house!" David Ames called back to Kathy as she followed him towards the front door. "Phone for an ambulance!"

Trembling she hurried to the phone in the hallway, Randall having ripped out the one in the kitchen. She was not sure what had happened. But she had heard the gritter rounding the bend. And she had heard Rick's scream. Thank God, Larry was caught up in the miracle of being able to see again. He gazed happily at the stuffed dog in his arms.

"You look just like I thought you would, Malcolm," Larry said complacently.

Kathy dialled the operator and reported the accident. She gave directions for reaching the house.

"The rescue squad will be there in minutes," the operator promised.

"Kathy . . ." Larry looked up. Puzzled. "Why was Randall here? Why did he try to hurt us?"

"Don't worry about that now, darling. You just stay here with Malcolm."

"Did Daddy shoot Randall?"

"No. He shot over Randall's head to try to make him stop. Randall ran in front of the gritter. He was hit." Larry would have to know. She took a deep, painful breath. "Larry, go see if the cake

213

is all burnt," she coaxed. "Turn off the gas, but don't touch the oven. Just look through the little window at the cake."

Standing behind the protection of the storm door, Kathy gazed outside. The floodlights spilt brightness all the way down to the road. The men from the gritter were leaning over Rick. No — Randall, she corrected herself. Larry had talked about Randall, who drove his tutor and him about town.

David Ames was out in the middle of the road, watching for the ambulance. The geese had finally ceased to honk. There was the ambulance now. David was beckoning to them.

The volunteers on the rescue squad jumped from the vehicle and swung into action. They put Randall onto a stretcher and lifted it into the ambulance. Then the ambulance rolled silently away, passing the approaching sleigh with Neil and the children.

David strode to the house while Neil helped the children from the sleigh to the edge of the road. Kathy could hear their exuberant goodnights to the farmer who drove the sleigh. Neil must have seen the ambulance. He must be anxious. Now he was talking to the men on the gritter. They would tell him what happened.

"He's dead," David reported softly as he walked into the house. "He was killed instantly."

"I can't believe it," Kathy whispered. "He followed Larry and me up from New York. On the Taconic he tried to push us off the road down into a gully. And three times before tonight he tried to kill Larry."

"It's all over," David comforted. "The whole nightmare is over."

"Daddy?" Larry's voice was sombre as he approached them. "Is Randall dead?"

"Yes, Larry," his father told him gently. "But it's better this way. He was very sick. Now he'll never be able to hurt anybody."

Neil was marshalling the children into the house now.

"Everybody up to the bedrooms to wash up and into pyjamas," Neil commanded briskly, though his eyes were bright with questions when they met Kathy's. "Then come back into the kitchen, and you'll have hot apple juice with cinnamon stirrers."

"We didn't ice the cake," Larry reminded Kathy. "It's kind of brown, but it isn't burnt."

"Ellie and you will ice it as soon as you come down in your pyjamas," Kathy promised. "Remember," she said, her face luminescent, "you don't need me to help you any more."

Larry threw his arms about his father's waist for a moment, and scurried after the others.

"Larry can see." David Ames' smile was dazzling. "I can't believe it!"

"It must have been the shock of what happened in his bedroom," Kathy said. "You were here, and he was so afraid for you. Knowing you were in danger, he was able to throw off the hysterical blindness."

215

"I want to know exactly what happened." Neil reached to take Kathy's hand in his as though to reassure himself that she was all right.

As briefly and as calmly as she could manage, Kathy gave Neil a replay of what had happened since he left the house with the children.

"He was after revenge on Anita." David's face was angry. "Anita and her young guys. Larry won't be exposed to Anita's behaviour any more. I mean to go into court and get custody of my son. I'm settling in New York. No more chasing around the globe. I want to see Larry every day of the week."

"How did you know where to find us?" Kathy was curious. "Did Martha tell you where we were?" Fate, she thought gratefully, that David Ames should arrive at that crucial moment.

"She couldn't find the address and she just knew that Larry and you were somewhere up-state. But she remembered that Sally Bevans had recommended the place, so I tracked down Sally. Martha was upset that you had called and said it was urgent to contact Anita. Even after she talked to Larry, she was worried." David took a deep breath. "Then I stopped for coffee down in Hoosick Falls. I heard a man talking about trouble with hunters up around here — and he said that someone up at the school had been hurt. I forgot the coffee and shot right up here."

Neil ruefully indicated the bandage on his scalp.

"It wasn't serious, but you couldn't have picked

a better moment to arrive." Neil strived for a humorous smile.

"Anyway, I figured if Larry and I couldn't spend Christmas together, we could at least celebrate New Year's together. I'll check into a motel close by."

"You'll stay here," Neil said firmly. "There's plenty of room."

Much later, with Larry half asleep in his father's lap before the Franklin stove and the other children sent off to bed for the night, Neil invited Kathy to join him on a visit to the geese.

"If I'm up late, I go out and take them corn." He chuckled. "They must be the most spoiled geese in the state. Also, the moon's out now. This time of month it's something special up here."

Kathy's eyes clung to his for an exhilarating moment.

"I'll go for a coat."

Hand in hand Kathy and Neil walked out the back door. They paused in silent appreciation of the magnificence of the view. The moon — incredibly large tonight — seemed to sit on top of the hill high behind the house.

"Neil, it's beautiful," Kathy murmured.

"You're beautiful." Neil pulled her into his arms.

The geese honked loudly. Kathy and Neil ignored them.

We hope you have enjoyed this Large Print book. Other G.K. Hall & Co. or Chivers Press Large Print books are available at your library or directly from the publishers.

For more information about current and up-coming titles, please call or write, without obligation, to:

G.K. Hall & Co.
P.O. Box 159
Thorndike, Maine 04986 USA
Tel. (800) 223-2336

OR

Chivers Press Limited
Windsor Bridge Road
Bath BA2 3AX
England
Tel. (0225) 335336

All our Large Print titles are designed for easy reading, and all our books are made to last.